I0761895

The Desert Store Series

Book #4

Susan Sugar Diamond

Away in a Desert

By Patsy Stanley

 This book is a work of fiction.

ISBN 978-1-7356266-0-4

Library of Congress Control Number

2020915716

About the Author

Patsy Stanley is an artist, illustrator, author and nature advocate. She has authored both nonfiction and fiction books including novels, children's books, energy books, art books, and more. She can reached at:

patsystanley123@gmail.com for questions and comments.

More books by Patsy Stanley:

Novels:

Addition Jones
An Older Wine
Emerald Hawks Flight
Avalon Blue's Quest

Illustrated books for all age readers:

Christmas Stories From the Crone's Castle
Big Al's Christmas Wedding
The Dreadful Noises of Landoshar

Native American:

Red Leaf
The Green Mountain Shaman

Metaphysical book Series:

The Mental Body
The Spiritual Nature of Atomic Structure
Sound Energies
Shield Energies
Chakras, Meridians, and the Color Energies
The Elements

The Desert Store Series:

Book One:
Cowboy Johnson's Desert Oasis
Mama and the '57 Mercury

Book Two:
The Red Cactus Desert
Geena and the '59 Dodge Lancer

Book Three:
The Three Cactus Limbo
Bud's Garage and the Quest of the Three Magi

Book Four:
Susan Sugar Diamond
Away in a Desert

Coming Soon! Book 5 in the Desert Store Series!

Table of Contents

Red ain't jist' a color, honee'
it's a place, a kon-dition, a time
a' angle, a jimble jamble, a rhyme
people likes or people's doan'
ya' sees what ah' means?

Part One

Normaine and Eddy

"This damn blizzard might stop us from leaving for the store when we planned," Eddy said ruefully, stomping the snow off his heavy black boots as he came in the back door of the large, spacious kitchen. He was carrying a giant pizza box. He kicked the door shut behind him with a booted foot.

"There isn't much stops a trucker, but this one looks pretty bad. May have to set it out."

"Yeah. I know," Normaine said. She was sitting at their long, wide wood kitchen table, dwarfed in the huge kitchen, listening to the latest weather forecast about the ongoing blizzard situation. The weatherman's voice sounded both excited and worried.

She was fiddling with a pair of pliers and a piece of wire. She was working on a metal mobile hanging from a long chain in the back of their cavernous warehouse-studio-apartment. The back area was filled with Normaine's art supplies, everything from rusty nails to paints to crystals to old, beat-up shoes. An uptown art gallery would arrive after the first of the year to collect mobiles for Normaine's one-woman art show.

Their apartment backed up to Napoliti's Pizza Parlor. Their tiny yard was divided by an alleyway between them and the next-door neighbors.

"Mama needs me."

Normaine's eyes were dark with worry. She looked at Eddy.

"Come here."

He bent down and kissed her noisily. She licked a snowflake off his handlebar mustache and looked him up and down. His brown eyes sparkled as he posed for her. Swarthy, short, and muscular, he was light on his feet and dapper like the Italian ancestors he sprang from. He preened at her admiring look, though he was holding a pizza box. Deftly, he slid the pizza box onto the table. She stood. They grabbed each other in an affectionate embrace and swayed back and forth.

"What would I do without you?' she asked worriedly.

"Don't borrow trouble, kiddo!"

"But Mama lost Cowboy Johnson too early! All of us did!"

"Nothing we can do about it now. Quit thinking about it and have some pizza before it gets cold."

Eddy shrugged out of his coat, hung it up and sat down at the table. He lifted the lid of the pizza box, grabbed a slice of pizza, slapped it on a plate, and handed it to Normaine. Then he took a slice for himself. A minute later, she asked, "Did they send any extra cheese?"

They ate in silence, staring out the window at the snow. From time to time, a gust of wind broke through the heavy downpour and they could see as far as the street. Yes, it was a hell of a blizzard.

The grief from losing Cowboy Johnson at the desert store last summer was always with them, though they tried not to show the depth of their pain in front of each other. The snow fell in steady, gusting waves, the wind blowing against the back door, causing it to rattle. Making it home to the desert store for their yearly Christmas gathering and Cowboy Johnson's memorial looked bleaker every minute.

After they finished eating, Eddy said, "Maybe you should call Mama and tell her we might be running late because of the blizzard. Maybe call her before the phones go out?"

Before she could pick up the phone to call, it rang.

"Hello?"

It was William. She listened while he talked.

"Oh, my God!" Normaine shouted. Eddy rushed to her side.

"What's going on?"

"William, tell Eddy what you just told me."

She handed the phone to Eddy and started circling the kitchen table.

Thank God there's no butcher knife out anywhere, Eddy thought, *or the table would be carved to ribbons She was safe with a chain saw, screwdrivers, and hammers, but not with a butcher knife.*

Eddy watched her while he listened to William.

"I understand," Eddy finally said into the phone. "I'm not surprised. Only surprised it didn't happen sooner."

He listened again.

"Okay. You're an honorable man, William, doing that for them. They're tough. They'll land on their feet. Not to worry. I will be here to help my three sisters settle back in. We'll just have to go to the desert store at a later time. I'll have Normaine call Mama and let her know. I'll call you back after while."

He hung up. Normaine shouted.

"I don't mind a visit from those dumbasses, but they're gonna' stay?"

"Yep. He's bought them an apartment, so at least they don't have to stay with us. They don't know about any of this yet."

"Thank God! So, they don't know this is a permanent visit?"

"Right."

"What about Christmas at the store?"

"They're coming here for Christmas, and we'll have to be the ones to help them settle back in. It should be easy since New York City is their home. Yeah. Thanks to William, they'll be in their own place! My God, the money it must have cost!"

Normaine rolled her eyes.

Eddy amended, “That'll make it a lot easier. We have to help, or they'll move in with us and make our lives hell! We'll have to go on the road and live there! William has to have help getting them off his back. I know how they are, and they'll make life a living hell for him and us too if we don't step in.”

Normaine assessed him with steady black eyes.

“So, we'll have to put up with them again.”

Eddy looked at the floor and sighed.

“At least not in our own house.”

Normaine snickered. “At least we got our own place now. No more Garage Bay Love! No more Hidden Nights of Love in Motel Room Four...or was it five or six or...all of them?”

Eddy grinned and rushed her. Pulled her into his arms. They smiled at each other, dark eyes sparkling.

“It's gonna' be one hell of a Christmas!” Eddy shouted, grabbing her face and kissing her. She pulled away from him.

“In a few minutes. I have to call Mama first.”

Geena and Ray

The snow fell in great, gusting sheets. Wind rippled over the tops of the pines, dusting snow onto their tops, then re-layering it. Geena stood watching the blizzard at a window in the huge, ornate living room. A log snapped in the fireplace, interrupting her thoughts. She turned from the window to look at Ray. He stood spread-legged before the large fireplace, his back to her, smoking his pipe, automatically posing as he stared down into the dancing flames. He looked every bit the fierce, darkly handsome picture of authority he believed he was. Many others believed it, too. She looked away, turning from that thought.

She could not bring herself to tease him about his aloofness to soften him. Her own newfound coolness prevented her. It permeated everything around her, not just him, as she'd once hoped. Sometimes she hated him. But she stayed, for she knew the things he did were not intentionally cruel. On his part, he stayed puzzled and limited about who she was and their relationship. These days she hurt him as often as he hurt her. Frustration and anger were the negative glues holding their relationship together. She thought it was so very different back in the beginning. Now, she realized it was always the same. Just a different place, a different setting. A different age. Still, there was something to be settled. Something that needed to be said.

"This blizzard is going to make any kind of travel impossible for at least the next few days, if not longer," she said carefully, watching him. After a considerable pause, he answered. "Yes. It's a big one. Looks like we might have to postpone our Christmas trip to the desert store."

There. It was out in the open. She didn't miss the hidden satisfaction in his voice. Geena nodded.

"Yes. Most likely."

She turned from the window and walked out of the room. He watched her leave. He knew she was going to Celia, who was nested in the library, reading yet another old tome. The library was Celia's home. She ate and paced and thought in the huge room filled with books. She came to him, filled with questions about what she read. He loved it. No complaints from him about crumbs on the tables, floor, or books. Smugly, he reveled in his authority, the position of greater knowledge he held with his daughter.

Goldie and Breck trailed after Geena. Ray studied the dogs. Golden Retrievers. Full-grown now. Both dogs ignored him and stayed away from wherever he was. He frowned. They should be used to him by now. He remembered grudgingly buying them as puppies for Geena and Celia. His mother ordered him to get them after she informed him he had a son, and she would keep that secret for him, but he would have to toe the mark with Geena and Celia. They were surprised and delighted to find the two golden, gamboling pups waiting for them when they came home to Ray from the desert store when summer ended. For a while, they fell back in love with him. Their gratitude for something they could love unconditionally lasted until his cold sophistication drove them away again. They never knew that his mother ordered him to buy the dogs and not tell them why.

Ray stared after Geena, puzzlement in his eyes. He expected her to put up a fuss about the possibility of cancelling the trip to the desert store. After all, it was supposed to be Cowboy Johnson's memorial Christmas gathering. He'd passed away last summer. That was months ago, and it wasn't like they weren't used to his absence by now. *Not something any of us are looking forward to anyway*, he thought resentfully. *Another wasted Christmas. I've got barely enough time available for the things I need to do as it is.*

He watched her slip out the door. Did anyone ever understand women? He sure as hell didn't. He glanced out the window with gratitude. The blizzard was timely. He never relished the yearly Christmas gathering at the desert store like the others did, though he pretended to with Geena and Celia and especially with Emma, who seemed to see beneath his surface to what he was hiding more easily each time he saw her. Which was why he avoided her.

He felt relief when he thought about not having to face the inquisition William the Dude, his grandfather, and the rest of the "misfits" put him through each year. He always came away lacking, feeling like a small boy who'd gotten a bad report card from the desert store bunch that called themselves misfits. They all disapproved of him. He had no idea why. Maybe it was because he wasn't a misfit. Maybe it was because he was highly educated, something most of them weren't.

Well, maybe he wouldn't have to go through it this year. He didn't want to have to face his grandfather or mother until they settled down a bit. Until their ruffled feathers smoothed out again. He knew they would keep his secrets; he wasn't worried about that. He just didn't want to put up with the humiliation he would surely have to endure from them. Or to worry again about his inheritance. Everybody else minded them because they were both rich as Croesus. For the first time, he wondered if they might pass him over in their wills in favor of his illegitimate son. Well, he'd throw a little sugar in the pot to make sure that didn't happen. His mother was a sucker for him. He'd figure out what and when.

He repeated what the excited weatherman was announcing.

"The biggest snowstorm to hit the east coast in years! All the way down from Maine through New York and as far south as the Carolinas! A blizzard of gigantic proportions!"

He smirked and took a long draw on his pipe. He could always pretend to be sick if the blizzard wasn't enough. He laughed inside with delight and relief.

Geena picked up the phone in the library and called Mama at the store.

"There's a blizzard here," she announced mournfully when Mama answered. Mama was silent for a moment, taking in what Geena was really saying.

"Okay."

Geena thought she sounded almost relieved.

"What's going on?" she asked suspiciously. Mama gave a short laugh.

"Oh, just this and that. Nothing to worry about," she said evasively.

"You're lying. Put Timmon on the phone," Geena ordered tersely.

"Okay. No problem."

In a minute, Timmon said, "Hello?"

"What's really going on?" Geena asked without preamble.

"Nothing I know anything about."

Geena narrowed her eyes.

"Both of you are lying. Why?"

Timmon stayed insistently evasive. Geena finally gave up. Whatever it was, they didn't want her in on it. She felt more alone than ever. She talked a few minutes more and hung up. She strode to a window to watch the falling snow. Oh God! Why couldn't she be someplace warm and kind, someplace where no one kept unkind, mean secrets? Someplace where they drove blue Nash Ramblers? Celia patted her arm.

“It’s okay, Mother. We’ll fit in later again.”

“What?” Geena asked her.

Celia touched her arm again.

“How about we bake some gingerbread cookies? Just plain round ones? I don’t like biting the heads off gingerbread men.”

“It looks like we’re not going home this Christmas. To the desert store, I mean. We’re not wanted,” Geena said. She glanced at Celia.

“I mean, we’re not supposed to.”

Celia studied her mother.

“I know. I knew yesterday. But this is one of our homes, too. And I like it very much for the bigness of it, plus Rudy, the fawn, has grown up in our woods.”

She nudged Geena’s attention back to the window. “There’s magic and plenty of Sight here, too, Mother. And Goldie and Breck like gingerbread almost as much as I do.”

Geena let go of her puzzlement and sadness. They hurried to the kitchen, holding hands.

That night, Geena dreamed. In the dream, she was thirteen again, and Cowboy Johnson was filling the gas tank of the woman in the little red car again. The woman looked straight at her and said insistently, “No, no, not Perry. Matthew.” Then the dream ended. She woke up in the morning knowing things had changed for the woman she’d briefly encountered just once years ago. Who the hell was Perry or Matthew?

She tried to go near this Matthew, to get a sense of his energy distantly and politely, to look at it, but he was too big and too angry and too loud. Too much energy to deal with. She'd hoped she'd never see that woman again, yet she'd dreamed about her. Go figure. Her Sight never erred. She trusted it completely. There was a reason she'd dreamed about the lady in the red dress. She'd find out later.

William "The Dude" Makepeace

William watched the black looks settle over the three Mafia sisters' faces. It was becoming all too clear that they were planning yet another vendetta against him and Timmon. Again and again and forever, it seemed.

But his wife Algestine's fruitcake still worked splendidly. It held all the healing powers of a world-renowned, mouthy, narcissistic traveling televangelist as it rode through his veins, landed at his joints and ladled soothing oil generously around them. Or a snake oil salesman. Or an "Ohmming" ventriloquist on the lam from a hidden monastery in Tibet, or Shamballa or some such place.

He sighed bitterly. He knew the source of his relief very well. It didn't travel. And it wasn't a pleasant one. Its name was Algestine. One of three sisters nicknamed "The Mafia Sisters" by Geena back in the good old days at the desert store.

The familiar suggestion crossed his mind for the umpteenth time. Maybe it was time to split up with Algestine. Time to go his own way again. She was tolerable until her sisters joined them in California. He and Timmon had plucked her two sisters from their nest at the desert store in New Mexico and brought them to California in desperation, hoping they would get Algestine's attention off of them. Big mistake. Instead of treating him with respect in front of them, she'd gone straight back to square one with a vengeance, proudly bossing him around, pouring it on thick when her bossy, admiring sisters were near. He usually just ambled off to any place they weren't when she started in. Yep. The Mafia sisters were back in business, and growing steadily worse.

Well, he didn't know how much longer he could take his body feeling better while who he was on every level got attacked on a daily basis whenever he was home. He and Timmon escaped at every opportunity. They visited all the vineyards in California and every tourist trap and fine restaurant up and down the west coast. They'd toured Seattle's sights, and they drove up to Alaska instead of flying to make the trip last longer.

Of course, the Mafia sisters didn't mind them not being around. They were all three bred in the bone natural spinsters that kept themselves busy haughtily advising the bewildered local Catholic priest on how to handle God, his personal business, and how to pray.

William knew he'd made a mistake within hours after he'd married Algestine and they'd left on their honeymoon. As soon as they reached Albuquerque, Algestine located the nearest Catholic Church and rushed off. She spent her time praying and trembling in fear whenever he came near her.

This was not the same woman who'd let him kiss her and fondle her large breasts and trim, sturdy body. Granted, she'd acted like the ancient virgin she was, and he'd expected to spend some time winning her over. To tell the truth, he was kind of looking forward to it, as he felt his age gave a good advantage to slow deployment of romancing her. Slow and steady. That's what he was looking forward to.

But it was not to be. He knew that now. Sometimes she decided to give in to his advances and came to him, presenting herself like a lamb being led to the slaughter. Her nightly behavior became repugnant to him, wearing thin his everlasting patience. At last he gave up and moved into a bedroom at the other end of the house to avoid her nightly maneuvers. She never mentioned his leaving her alone in their private suite, but he could see the relief written on her face. He decided it was her privilege to stay a virgin so she could be high on Christ's waiting list to get into heaven. Mission accomplished. Love lost.

He turned from her and hid his deep well of yearning and desire to make love with a woman who truly wanted and valued him. That hadn't happened for him since Andrea. Beautiful, darkly sad, pessimistic Andrea, whose windswept hair still floated around him in his dreams along with the gentle voice of his daughter Emma's lovely, dearly departed mother.

His heartbreak and disappointment sometimes overwhelmed him. During those times, he went to see Lily Jean Bloome to get his astrology chart updated and to have his fortune looked over. Those things were merely tools. They just gave him an excuse to spend time with her.

Lily Jean Bloome had gone through her own hells of endurance and misery when she was young. Though her daughter still suffered from the ravages of childhood sexual abuse and her sons were anxiety-ridden and angry, she'd eventually found peace. She'd accepted that she couldn't fix them, that they'd always lay the blame for their misery at her doorstep. She distanced from them little by little until she made a life alone for herself, one in which their constant blame stayed distant enough for her to ignore.

He admired her. He went to see her the first time on an impulse. It was after Timmon told him about seeing her and having his fortune read.

"She's a sort of psychic. But I think of her as just a very kind woman. Real nice. One who doesn't have a need to kick all men's asses."

William knew Timmon was referring to the three Mafia sisters and their never-ending vendetta against them. He was intrigued. Maybe there were more unexplored paths to finding the soothing spiritual peace he craved than he thought. Maybe this was one. An optimist filled with unmet needs, William began to wonder if this Lily Jean Bloome person would be able to see past his façade, his kind, mild old man mannerisms, down to his intense and deeply buried feelings. He glanced up at Timmon, who stood waiting, studying his face.

"Want her phone number?" Timmon asked.

"Well, dog my cats! I guess somethin' needs to be done."

Timmon nodded.

"It does."

He removed a neatly folded piece of paper from his pocket and handed it to William. William grinned at him.

"Pretty desperate, are you?"

"Yes," Timmon said. We've run out of orchards, and viable backwoods retreats to inspect."

William grinned.

"Me too."

They both knew what he was talking about. The misery they lived in had to stop or it would kill them both off. Timmon nodded and turned away. William picked up the phone and called the number written on the small piece of paper.

Desperately trying to be positive and feel something besides old again, he dressed carefully in clean, pressed blue jeans and a pale blue shirt he hoped enhanced his sky blue eyes. He rolled the sleeves up on the crisp shirt and grinned at his longish white hair. It was a good shade of white, like pure white snow on a mountain top. Then he slid on his neon green flip flops.

Following an impulse, he drove his vintage truck to his first appointment with Lily Jean Bloome. He parked, got out, and looked his canary yellow 1946 half-ton GMC truck over fondly. He and Avery had enjoyed many a ride in it and downed many a cold, frosty beer in it. But that was over now. Forever. He sighed heavily and turned away. In front of him were a few shaded, wide wood steps leading down to a corner. He went down the steps, turned a corner, and knocked on the door of the beach cottage.

He looked around while he waited. A sign announcing this was home sweet home hung above an arched stone doorway. Pale yellow walls of large stone, adobe, and red brick surrounded him on three sides, with one side open to a splendid view of beach and ocean, allowing the scents and sounds of beach and water to curl up inside the open entryway like a clever blue cat drowsing there.

Vegetables grew around him, flourishing in adroitly placed nooks and crannies and in copper pots and clay pans in the dappled sun and shade. They were mixed in with wildflowers, little figures of animals, fairies, elves, gnomes, and little people. The combination should have been confusing, but it somehow exuded a peaceful magic. For one thing, there were planned negative spaces here, too. He could tell. After all, his daughter was Emma Makepeace, a famous artist. Shade and sunshine were well known and well planned for. They were tended to, just as carefully as one would tend a saint in their care. The combination made the place feel holy.

Although it was the hottest part of the day, it was cool down here. He sighed. Something in him began to relax. It was hard to relax with constant pain complaining its way through his joints. He shook his head. He hadn't been surrounded by magic like this in a while, though he knew magic well enough to know it generally turned up in the most unexpected of places. Just like in this little unexpected corner of the world.

He turned as the door opened. Time spun to a stop as he gaped at the woman standing there. She was older than anybody ever would be and younger than a child at the same time. No wonder Timmon couldn't describe her. How could anyone? She was ageless, one of those rare women who would never know how very beautiful she was, always was, and always would be. A flower blooming, waiting, not looking forward nor backward, just waiting for the next thing life handed her to deal with, not fighting the changes life wrought upon her, just staying who she was.

That was the thing. Transparency. She was Light. Light shone through her, telling it all. Her history. How she felt about the worlds she'd lived in before this age and the world she lived in now. He guessed she stood about five four or thereabouts. Maybe four or five inches shorter than him. Soft and curvy where he was thin and bony. A comfort to his mind to think there might be a sheltering place for his weary bones, aching and screaming at times for rest.

Her clothes were too big for her. He imagined they made her look fat to some people, people not in the know. People who didn't know about hair waterfalls to hide behind. People who'd never met someone like Geena and Mama back at the desert store, an energy vortex, a place that attracted different kinds of Seers. There were people who didn't know that a belt buckle could be a shield, and a tent to hide in could be easily worn, disguised as clothes. They might scoff at the kingdom he now stood in.

Yep... time to back off and reconnoiter ...his last thought as he was somehow swept through the arched door. Later, he remembered the kindness of the pale green color of the door. He heard the whispered closing of it behind him, leaving him standing in a new place of promise. There was no time to back off now. Never was, really. He was too old to wait any longer.

"Come in," Lily Jean Bloome said, fine white wild-haired, strong, long chinned, wide-faced as an open book.

"I have frozen black sweet cherries in the freezer and a rocking chair for you to rest in. They'll help your arthritis."

His mind flew back to a soul-sick and diminished young boy whose mother tried to feed him frozen cherries, and the brother who'd raged at his mother to stop because he wanted the boy to die. The mother had handed him the bowl of cherries and gone to his brother and left him alone. He'd survived. But the pain of it lived in his very bones. He didn't bother asking how this woman knew. It was enough that she did.

He glanced around the large, mostly empty pale yellow room. Floor-length, sheer white curtains flowed in the warm, salt-laden breeze drifting lazily through the many large open windows facing the ocean. A comforting, steady, distant hum through them announced the ocean's activities. She looked into the air, seeing something. She frowned and shook her head.

"There are no demon's here to stop you from eating the frozen cherries this time, thus taking down your internal fever, at last. No, not this time." She shook her head firmly and took his hand, drawing him gently further into the shade in her home to rest.

His first visit was a catalyst. He left from it with his mind made up. Lily Jean Bloome didn't make it up for him. His body and soul did. He'd always enjoyed his gift for living in the moment. In the worst of life's earthquakes, he was always able to stand in the rain under an umbrella and enjoy Nature. Looking back over the past few years, he realized that the basic life core of him, the living one who absolutely knew he was a part of Nature, was disappearing. If he wanted to live much longer, it was time to get it back. Make it strong again. Strengthen it.

He began stalking a new life plan, examining and studying ways and means. New meanings took place in him as the colors and layers of his life shifted. In the end, it came down to acknowledging to himself that kindness was generally wiser than truth. He'd been had, took to the cleaners, but it was of his own making. Being bitter over it wouldn't get him anywhere but dead.

The three Mafia sisters were going to New York City to visit relatives while he went to the desert store for the annual Christmas gathering of misfits. That was the plan. He didn't ask the sisters to return to the store with him. He didn't want them there ever again. His grief over Cowboy Johnson's passing was a private, never-ending pain, an internal howling, keening match for his arthritis.

He knew his emotional pain would escalate when he was back at the store, and he knew he needed to stay calm and take care of Mama and Geena. Those two had called Avery "Cowboy Johnson" with more love in their voices than any man had a right to. Every man except Avery, who'd done without his share of love too long before they showed up at his little church-store in the New Mexico desert.

Mama and Geena were first on the agenda. He prayed the time that was left before Christmas would carry him to a new place where his grief over Avery wasn't so raw. He accepted without rancor that time does heal. Distance and time.

Thank God for the red cactus desert! He planned to spend plenty of time there. Whatever time there was left to him on this Earth, he needed to spend it more wisely. Time itself wasn't finite, but his personal time was. He couldn't wait things out anymore like he used to. His priorities needed to change.

"Any of you take a notion to go back to the desert store with me for Christmas, just let me know," he informed the sisters perversely, knowing the sisters hated being at the desert store and never wanted to see it again.

"No. We're going to New York to spend time with our relatives," Algestine answered for the three of them in a cold, emphatic voice. The other two nodded. All three of them turned their black-clad backs to him. He grinned at their backs morosely and ambled away. He was keeping his own secrets now, and they were good ones.

He did what he could with the situation. He bought an apartment for the sisters to live in. Ground floor. Large and shockingly expensive. His lawyers would offer it to them after they were in New York, and see what they said, never doubting they would take it. After all, there was a prenup. Thank God for that!

He knew life wasn't easy for the three old spinsters. They needed familiar surroundings and to be close once more to the church they'd attended since childhood back in New York City. They'd ridden out into the world with Eddie, leaving the cozy, righteous routines of their lives behind. Eddie was in love, and they never gave a thought to anything but sacrificing for their only brother. They'd sacrificed for him at every opportunity all their lives. Eddy didn't always appreciate their efforts. But they ignored him and did what they thought to be right. After all, he was the only son and the baby of the family.

They'd given up their rigid, grim routines when Eddie asked them to be his chaperones on the road. They took the train to Dakota, then left town with him in Esmerelda, wending their way south through heat and dust and people with strange accents, odd people without an iota of knowledge about cleanliness being next to godliness. Like old-time missionaries, set in their ways, bringing their cleanliness is next to godliness version of saintliness to lost souls. That was the whitewashed version, William thought grimly, brushing aside sentimentality in favor of reality.

The three Mafia sisters didn't know they wouldn't be returning to California after spending Christmas in New York. They would find out through the lawyers in New York. He was too much of a coward to face their contempt, anger and wrath in person. They'd slice him into verbal ribbons if he told them the truth face to face. This was better. Timmon was surprised, then relieved, when William told him. They met in William the Dudes office.

"I didn't think you'd ever ditch her," Timmon said. "I mean, separate from her."

"Well, I will just have to find a way to get on without her fruitcake." William sighed ruefully.

Timmon's blue eyes widened.

"Are you serious?"

"Yes. It's been a hard decision to make, but I believe I will live longer putting up with my arthritis pain than I will if I keep putting up with the three of them."

William sighed again and looked at Timmon for confirmation. He watched Timmon's gentle, mild, tan face grow redder and redder until he finally burst out laughing.

"What's so funny?" William asked.

"You. Ha ha! I took her damned fruitcake to a lab and got it tested a long time ago, hoping this day would come! I have the results in a folder in the locked bottom drawer of a desk! I know what's in the damn fruitcake! Ha hah ha!"

William was astounded.

"That's not exactly ethical, is it?"

"No more than her holding you hostage over a piece of damned fruitcake! I got Lily Jean Bloome to make batches of it to test on the old folks over in The Foundation Nursing Home. Somehow, some of them are getting easier to live with, and are almost on the edge of enjoying life again! Ha ha ha!"

Timmon doubled over in merriment. He guffawed and slapped his knee when William's jaw dropped.

"Fly catcher!"

Timmon accused, pointing his finger at William, his beautiful blue eyes merry in his tan face, his even white teeth gleaming. William admired his handsome face and athletic young build for an instant.

"Was that the right thing to do?"

Timmon smirked.

"I'm confused."

"You have been, right from the start, I think."

Timmon smirked again, wiping tears of laughter from his eyes with the back of his hand. He pointed his finger at William.

"A rich, philosopher guy like you is a sitting duck for an old female dictator with large bohunkas, a smarmy smile, and a loaf of souped-up bread!"

Timmon threw his hands out in a sudden "hold it" gesture.

"Wait here! I'll be right back!"

He strode out of the room. In a short time, he returned, holding a manila file folder. He handed it to William. William opened it and studied the blessed written release from both his short-sightedness and his arthritic pain.

"Thank you, Timmon. I should have thought of this myself, but damn glad you did. The keys to my freedom at last! I'm putting you in charge of every aspect of this venture. And while you're at it, have the lab analyze those other two devil's fruitcakes, too! The men that come around seem to be addicted to them."

"Yeah, like they have heroin or something in them!"

They both laughed, then stared at each other thoughtfully.

William called Eddy and Normaine to tell them the Mafia sisters' visit was going to be permanent.

"Oh, my God!" Normaine shouted into the phone. He jerked the receiver away from his ear.

"I don't mind a visit from those dumbasses, but they're gonna' stay?"

"Yep. I bought 'em a place up there they don't know about yet."

"So, they don't know this is a permanent visit?"

"Right."

Silence ran down the phone lines. Normaine mulled it over while William waited. At last, she said, "You bought em' a place? They're not gonna' move in on us?"

"Right," William said.

"Well, bring Satan's helpers on! But I gotta' ask why."

William answered, "Well, Normaine, sometimes my emotional pain gets stronger than my arthritis pain. And I have to pick and choose. I'm a slow learner and a slow mover. I guess it's better late than never."

"Did ya' ever get the recipe?"

"Timmon got it for me."

Normaine laughed.

"Here's Eddy. Give him the glad tidings."

After he hung up, he thought about Lily Jean Bloome. He wondered if it was too soon to visit her again. He shook his head to clear it. He stayed of two minds about her, but his advanced age sensibly urged him to take advantage of all the true caring he could find before he croaked out.

He longed to touch a real woman again with tenderness and kindness and have it returned. He craved the feel of an older woman's warm skin, skin smelling like only a woman's could. He wanted lips brushing his with sedate exploration and a willingness to give what they could. That was a large part of why he'd married Algestine. Well, it was over, and given his age, he was grateful to be able to plan any future without her.

"Timmon, I need you to head out to the desert store and stay with Mama. She's gonna' need you again. I've got a feeling all that's gonna' change and free you up, but I don't know exactly when or how. How does that set with you?"

Timmon grinned.

"I've already booked my flight into Albuquerque."

William studied him. Timmon grinned back at him.

"I'm going to need a raise if I have to keep taking care of you old folks," Timmon said. They both chuckled.

William grimaced. There was something else to take care of. It was time to call Perry and tell him about Mama's secret, crazy, stubborn idea of heading to California in the spring to somehow avenge Avery. He knew about it because Hector and Annie called him weekly to update him on how Mama was doing. They said she was slowly wasting away. Slowly moving left of center.

He called her every day to try and stem the tide. But she was becoming absent-minded during her conversations with him. He had no idea what new, goofy plans she was busy thinking up, but he knew she was headed in the general direction of getting herself into big trouble. Yep. It was time. What he planned might give her something to hold on to. Or drive her further out. He mentally checked the time there was left to work with. Not much. Only three weeks 'til Christmas.

Timmon was heading back to the desert store tomorrow. He'd meet him out at the ranch three days before Christmas. He needed to cut it that close because of his plan to get rid of the Mafia sisters. He sighed. Maybe everybody would settle in with Mama, and it would all work out okay. Maybe. He sure as hell hoped so. He remembered what people said about "the best laid plans"...going awry.

"Well, dog my cats!" he muttered.

Mama

She slid the battered overnight bag from its hiding place under the cot and placed it beside the cardboard file box containing Cowboy Johnson's journals and legal papers. She'd discovered the overnight bag at a used store in Albuquerque, sitting just inside the open door, waiting for her. It wasn't an accident. She'd seen it when she walked by. It looked like an ugly, squat toad with spots sitting in the sunshine, waiting for her. The sight of it instantly took her back to a warm sunny day when she and a twelve-year-old girl escaped from prison by setting out on the road with her small savings tucked inside a huge, ugly purse that looked like a first cousin to the overnight bag. She'd turned into the store, grabbed it in a death grip, and bought it.

Now it sat at her feet, aged, ragged, and spotty, packed and ready to help her escape again, like she did all those years ago. She grabbed the urn from its place under Cowboy Johnson's cot, cradled it in her arms and paced the floor. She talked to him until the outside light dimmed toward night.

It was after seven in the evening, but the daylight lingered. Shadows were gathering in the silent, deserted store. The whispering would start soon. It was time to leave. Hector and Annie, the store helpers, went home after fixing her dinner and fussing over her not eating enough. The cold chicken salad and green beans sat untouched in the refrigerator. Hector and Annie wouldn't be back until morning.

She shook her head no without realizing what she was doing. She wouldn't let them have him. Not yet. She loved them, but he belonged to her. He was hers. Forever and always. She didn't want to share him with them, and she wouldn't. Probably never. That's the way it was. She loved him the most.

She sat the urn down and picked up the file box and carried it through the store and out to the Merc'. She opened the back door and stashed it on the floorboard. Then she went back in and picked up the urn in one hand, then leaned down and gripped the handles of the squat, rustic overnight bag with her other hand. It banged against her leg. She walked through the living quarters in the back of the once upon a time church-store and through the front, knowing it would be a while before she came back here again, if ever. She looked at books and shelves and counters and popsicles, waiting for them to intercede with memories to stop her leaving, but they didn't. She set the urn down on the front service counter and laid the worn, small slip of paper on the counter. It read, 'I'll be back in a few days."

She hoped the note was a big, fat lie. She needed more than just a few days. Besides, she wasn't actually running away, she told herself. If she stayed here, she would die. The memories of Cowboy Johnson still overpowered every inch of the place. It was just too hard to take any longer. She picked up the urn, walked out the front door, set the bag down, and locked the door behind her. She hurried down the front porch steps to the Merc' and opened the passenger door. With one hand she tossed the bag in, shut the door and walked around to the driver's side. She opened the door and set the urn just so on the floorboard to keep it from possibly falling over.

It felt like a century passed before she was settled into the car. She turned the key in the ignition and the Merc' purred to life, ready for another road trip. Anywhere. Any time. Let's go. She turned out onto the highway and carefully drove north. A different direction than last time. But still, away from the desert store. She was running away to keep him. To survive.

She'd been warned in her dreams. The huge, hulking, frowning, shouting bad man was coming to take all that was left of Avery away from her. Another younger man entered later dreams. He wasn't as bad as the first man, but they looked alike. Almost identical, except for size and sound. The younger man was quiet. Both men resembled Cowboy Johnson. The resemblance was unmistakable. Both men wanted the same thing—to get Avery back. To take him away from her and everyone else he'd ever belonged to. They'd do it legally if they didn't get their way. They'd make their move over Christmas.

She wrestled with knowing it would happen without telling anyone for weeks, trying to figure out how to change the certainty of her dream. Being psychic held its drawbacks, but this time, she needed to make it work for herself instead of somebody else. She needed to leave the sacred place the store was and find another sacred place to be powerful from.

She inched along the blacktopped highway until she reached the almost unnoticeable, thin, dusty stream of a path on the right side of the blacktop. She made an exacting right turn on it, slow as a snail. After a while, she rode underneath the familiar curved iron ranch sign.

The compound came into view. She drove past it and parked the Merc' behind it, out of sight. She got out, grabbed the urn, retrieved the worn bag, and headed for the back door.

Emma opened the door. Mama was not surprised. Emma had the Sight, too. So did Geena. And Timmon. Emma waited for her to enter. Mama brushed past her. Emma followed her all through the house while she searched and finally found a safe place to light. She lit in the laundry room. Emma knew why she chose it. It was the smallest room in the house. White and clean. A place where dirt got dealt with. A place where cleaning products lined the shelves and sunlight sparkled through bright, clean windows. Mama sat down, white-faced, exhausted and looked at Emma.

"They're coming to the store to take him away from me! I can't let it happen! I'm staying here!"

The words burst out of her. She dropped the bag and clutched the urn so tight her knuckles whitened.

Emma studied her. She was pale and thin enough to almost see through. This woman couldn't go on much longer. She studied the chased silver urn, round and dignified in quiet beauty. Just like Cowboy Johnson always was. No scrolls or fillers there. Just the best of lines converging and joining forces to hold the remains of a dear friend. Tears studded her eyes.

Still holding the urn, Mama jumped up and lunged toward her. They embraced each other and cried. After a while, Mama sat the urn down.

"Oh my lord. What are we gonna do?" Mama asked plaintively.

Emma sighed.

"We need to find a vase..." her voice trailed off. The solution might be that simple. She hurried to the kitchen with Mama trailing behind her. She'd seen that same vase shape before. In fact, there was more than one in her house. Same color, same shape. Filled with flowers, dried or fresh. That was good. *Keep em' guessing,* Emma thought. Mama interrupted her focus.

"It was my idea to have them all share in dispersing his ashes this Christmas. Now, I don't wanna' do it... no! I won't do it! Then the dreams...of the two men... They're coming to the store to try to take away what little I have left of him!"

"Quiet for just a minute, ok? I have to think," Emma said. They both stopped and stood still in the quiet. Emma thought swiftly. At least Mama had finally blasted herself out of the desert store. Thank God for that! She'd been killing herself wallowing in the memories surrounding her there. Now what to do? She tuned into Mama's words and looked. One of the men was a taker. The other was not. But they shared common grounds. Legal stuff. Genetics and something more. Maybe they were relatives. She shrugged the Seeing away. Later. One step at a time.

Emma Makepeace

I've always needed hideouts, Emma thought. *I always will.*

There were plenty of them in the compound. And in the guesthouses. And in the garage and stables. And out back in the fence row. Little hidden nooks and crannies built in here and there and everywhere. William didn't ask any questions when she added her hideouts to the original building plans. He just stepped back and studied her awhile after she added the first one.

"Puts me in mind of your mother. She was like that, too, you know."

When any of the workers questioned the purpose of so many hidey holes, William answered for her.

"No purpose. Haven't got any. Just makes the place more mysterious and charming."

The way he stated the words stopped any further questions. Mama hid out in the tiny bedroom behind the laundry room. She stored the urn under the bed and carried in the box with Cowboy Johnson's journals in it. The scruffy bag holding her clothes came in last.

The next afternoon, Mama called Geena and Ray, then Normaine and Eddy, with Emma standing patiently by to help explain if she needed it. She didn't mention where she was, and they didn't ask. That told her they already knew. She supposed Annie and Hector or somebody probably called them. Or Emma. She handed Emma the phone.

"It's probably best you're snowed in and not able to spend Christmas at the store. Mama is staying here with me for now. At least she's out of the store and in a new place where she can heal some more. She loves you, but she can't bring herself to share his ashes or disperse them yet. It just isn't time."

They were all relieved.

"Don't waste your time feeling guilty. It's supposed to be this way. Please stay safe and enjoy your Christmas. We'll make new plans. We will probably get together in the spring. We can have a Christmas tree then."

"I'll call Bud, Ben and Andy later." Mama said. Emma nodded and left. Mama never mentioned the dreams of the two men who would inevitably arrive at the store for Christmas to anyone she called.

Emma hung another Christmas ornament on the tree before she turned and strolled to the window and looked out, not seeing the blowing sand or tumbleweeds. Mama was practically living in the small, hidden bedroom behind the laundry room. She spent hours pacing from the bed to the chair to the window holding the urn with Cowboy Johnson's—Avery's—ashes in it. Almost a week of hiding out in the little room, leaving it only to go to the kitchen and grab something to eat or to talk to Timmon when he came to visit. *Oh well. The situation will play itself out somehow.*

She turned back to the partially decorated tree and resumed humming Christmas carols and decorating. She decorated until the branches were loaded with angels. On the surface, Emma's personality was cool and sparse, with a few strong lines needing a minimum of necessary connection with people and things. But underneath her cool exterior and shyness lay a strong, passionate nature that showed up in the colors and lines of her paintings. She tried to hide it, but it stalked her at night in her bedroom high in the compound, causing her to unlock her secret library door, go in and delve into the romance novels she would never let herself live out in real life. Her secrets stayed hidden from the public, but Christmas was the one place she allowed a few close people to see her openly practicing excess.

She hummed under her breath. Company was coming. Well, an unexpected turn of events wasn't going to stop her from celebrating the unseen angels, guides, and beings that helped her soul's journey through this life. She loved them with all her heart. She loved placing angels and gnomes and elves and all manner of little folk here and there and everywhere and honoring them each year at Christmas. They were her best friends. Always were.

She tried to persuade Mama to help, but Mama was focused on reading the journals in the boxes she'd carried from the trunk of the Merc' and stored under the bed in the hidden little bedroom.

Mama waited until Emma was gone from the house before she scurried to the phone in the kitchen and dialed a number. A deep male voice answered.

"Brother Tom," the voice said. "Can I help you?"

She knew his question was not just rhetorical.

"I need to talk to Bud Spinner at 6:10 a.m. tomorrow morning. Tell him it's Map Girl. I'll call him back then."

She hung up the phone before the man could answer. The kitchen would be empty at that early hour. Emma slept upstairs at the back of the house. William slept downstairs at the back of the house. The guest rooms were back there, too. The kitchen help came in later. She'd been here long enough to know their schedule. She hurried back to the little bedroom to pack and plan.

The next morning, she called Bud. He answered. In a low voice she said, "Come and get me. Leave at this exact time two days from now. I'm going back to the monastery with you and stay for a while. Bring Ben and Andy with you. See if you can get me a good energy place, maybe a chapel sort of place to stay in. I need to heal. I need you three Magi's to come and get me."

"Okay," he said.

"Here's the number. Call from someplace and let the phone ring once when you're an hour or so away, then hang up. I'll be ready. Let the phone ring just once. Drive up to Emma's back door. I'll be waiting for you outside."

She hung up.

Emma's phone rang later that day.

"Is William there? I need to speak with him without Mama around."

Emma recognized Dan's voice.

"I'll have him call you back." She hung up. Soon William was at the desert store and on the phone with Dan Swain.

"I drove to the store so we could have privacy to talk. Mama's staying out at the ranch so we can't talk there. Okay. You can talk freely now, Dan. Spill the beans," William said. Dan snickered.

"Remember how I told you Matthew Mark Judson was thinking about coming to the desert store for Christmas?"

"Yes."

"So, there's another little Christmas surprise for you. Comin' right on that one's heels. Like a bob-tailed cat. Like dust behind a covered wagon."

William was used to Dan's need to use metaphorical phrasing when he got emotionally involved with anything. For an instant, William wondered what Dan's women were forced to listen to when he got wound up.

"Bud Spinner called me," Dan said. "Mama called him and asked him to come and get her. He's going to pick up Mama and take her back to the monastery to stay for a while. Bud and Ben and Andy are supposed to keep it a secret. The three Magi will do a drive-by at Emma's about 2 o'clock day after tomorrow to pick Mama up. Better be at the store or somewhere else. You and Emma."

"Well, dog my cats! Let me think for a minute."

“Sure.”

Bud laid the phone down. Timmon picked it up.

“How are you, Mr. Swain?” Timmon asked cheerfully.

“I’m fine, Timmon. Just gave William a bit of surprising news,” he said with a hint of glee.

“Timmon laughed. “We’ve been getting lots of that around here lately, Mr. Swain.”

Two days later, at two o’clock in the afternoon, Mama heard the phone in the kitchen ring once. She waited exactly a half an hour before she grabbed up the overnight bag and the file box with Cowboy Johnson’s urn in it and snuck through the kitchen with them. She tossed the note saying she was leaving for the monastery with Bud, Ben, and Andy on the counter. She set her things outside, closed the door behind her, and waited. In a few minutes, Bud drove up in the old black 30’s coupe he’d restored years ago. Ben was riding shotgun. Andy was in the back. Mama tossed her suitcase in, then slid the file box with Cowboy Johnson’s journals and urn in. Andy grabbed them and made room for Mama on the backseat.

Emma kept decorating and humming as she watched Bud’s car creep slowly past the living room windows. She grinned and went to the phone to call William at the store.

“She’s made good her escape. You can come home now. The three Magi will tell her we know, so she doesn’t feel bad for fleeing. She’s a bit under the weather and needs a healing place—this is a smart move—and the three Magi's gentleness."

"Well, dog my cats," William said.

The car purred along, nice and warm inside. *A good car likes a good road trip,* Bud thought. Bud studied Mama through the rearview mirror. She was asleep. She was smaller and paler than he remembered. She looked like the pictures in the books Ben read now. Like a child's dream of an earth fairy—they were always old—only without wings. She looked as though a strong wind would blow her away. Her large, lovely waif's eyes were closed in trust and sweet sleep. He remembered her as a little girl, chewing gum. She had the Sight and the Light and wings way back then, too. He'd taken care of her back then, he'd take care of her now. He glanced at Andy, then at Ben. They looked back at him. They would keep the vigil, too.

Mama dreamed. She sat on the campfire log Cowboy Johnson always sat on. He was bigger than her; most people were. Especially lately. She sighed and thought wistfully about the things she'd never do now. Geena and Celia would have to go on without her. So would the rest. But Cowboy Johnson had made all of them strong, including her. She could do this.

She remembered being a brown-haired, skinny girl who married a monster and ran away from him in her '57 Mercury. She remembered Geena hiding from life behind her long, thick, straight brown hair. She thought of Normaine and Eddy and the good, tough love they shared and would forever. William was finally with his mate. All was well with them.

For some reason, Cowboy Johnson was drawing two generations of Judson's to the desert store for Christmas, plus the two women who would change those men's lives. Admiration flashed through her for his quiet, humbling power and steadfast reach.

Suddenly it started snowing. Puzzled, she opened her eyes and looked out the car window. A figure came towards her through the odd, falling snow. She threw her arms out in greeting when she saw who it was. At last! She'd managed to hold on until he came for her. She slept again.

When she woke up, Bud looked at her and said nervously, "We don't aim to bother you, Map Girl, but Brother Tom has arranged it. A special place for you to stay, I mean. We hope it is what you asked for. Small and sort of sacred, I mean. It has flowers and stained glass windows, like your atrium at the store."

"Uh huh," Ben and Andy nodded.

Mama smiled a luminous smile at them. Her smile reminded Bud of the books he'd read and the art he'd seen describing the Madonna's smile. It was that kind of smile.

"We left at exactly 6:10 a.m. yesterday. The phone lines were out. We've driven since then. We also hauled along a snowmobile on a small trailer behind us just in case of more snow."

"I'm not going back there."

She closed her eyes.

Bud cleared his throat. Ben and Andy began to hum softly. Mama was their Map Girl too, now. After today, she no longer belonged to the desert store or to its people anymore. They would tell her later that everyone knew she was leaving, and out of love, they'd let her go. They all knew she must leave the desert store or die.

William knew it too. Now was not the time to tell her or the three Magi that Avery didn't need to be avenged any more. Mama had the Sight, and she might see what they knew and was keeping secret. She was still a badass that way. Better that she had a purpose in life again. To heal, then to go after Avery's enemies. She needed to see herself as an avenging angel so she could live again. Let her dream of vanquishing a formidable foe when she couldn't kill a piss ant or a bug these days. When she was well again, he would tell her and the three Magi the truth. Or someone would.

Timmon

Hector and Annie picked Timmon up at the Albuquerque airport. They were happy and relieved to see him. They laughed and filled him in on events on the ride back to the desert store. He would have rented a car, but Hector and Annie liked picking him up, and he liked letting them. Besides, riding down the road, people told plenty more than they would have in a more formal setting.

As he climbed out of their dusty old truck, he flashed for an instant back to the first night he'd spent here. He was ten years old and all mixed up back then. His crazy mother, who had the Sight, who chose to walk the dark side of life, and his crazy sisters eventually demonized him to the point that there was no choice but to estrange from them. He never saw or spoke to them again. As far as he knew, his father and two older brothers were still in prison.

Those bad old days were over. He wasn't curious about his family, and he never yearned after any of them. He remembered their evils too well. If the time ever came when he wanted to know anything, he'd contact Dan Swain or another detective. He shook his head, grabbed his suitcase from the truck bed, and bounded up the porch steps.

He took them two at a time, then waited for Hector and Annie to catch up. He hovered over them, grinning while they unlocked the door. Following them inside, he looked around and sucked in a deep, satisfying breath of familiar desert store air. It was always the same. Loaded with scents of bread, sour pickles, peppermint, onions, and all manner of nifty things, the store always smelled wonderful. The desert store air smelled like nowhere else he'd ever been. He'd sniffed and sorted through the heavenly myriad of odors during his first days here.

Yes, he'd fallen into the arms of a safe haven- Heaven on Earth- when he stumbled in terror through this door as a ten-year-old. He'd grown up here. Wised up, too, with the help of the misfits living at the store back then. They'd taught him the opposite things he was learning from his family. They taught him about honor and respect. Love. Liking. Working hard. Keeping your nose clean. He loved all of them, for they'd given freely of their hugs and affection to his starving, bewildered soul and kept it alive. He'd learned to make wind chimes and rag rugs along with the basics of scalping somebody with Normaine. Eddy taught him to dance and that women were admirable and to be looked up to. William taught him how to develop his Equanimity while they panned for gold a week at a time off in the desert hills. Mama baked him countless piles of peanut butter cookies. Cowboy Johnson's steady, quiet presence healed the fears of abandonment that rose whenever he made a mistake. The three Mafia sisters taught him how to make fruitcakes and how to rest his head properly on their heavily padded chests while they prayed over him.

Timmon liked the memories that came as he crossed the long length of the store into the living quarters in the back. They were old friends. He set his suitcase down and went out the back door. He stood on the back porch, looking around. This place was his home. Cowboy Johnson saved his life. So did Mama and all the others who lived here back then. He smiled, strolled back inside and closed the door.

The next morning over breakfast, he got busy sorting things out. Making plans. Thinking it through. *"Okay. Emma, William, and Lily Jean Bloome were staying out at the ranch. Mama has fled."* He grinned. He was relieved that he wouldn't have to deal with her. Their Sights bumped into each other at times, and he didn't understand her. He was too young, he knew.

"Well, good for her! Sometimes he felt like fleeing too. Okay. Back to business. Perry will be arriving at the store God knows when, any time from now until Christmas. The motel rooms must be inspected, cleaned, and made ready for whoever was coming. And there was more than just Perry coming."

He was staying in the back room, sleeping on Cowboy Johnson's cot because it still smelled like him. Wryly, he shook his head. His olfactory perceptions were so acute he was constantly offered ridiculously high paying jobs by perfume makers and winery professionals. Well, so much for inheriting the Sight from his evil mother. The third eye, just above the nose, had everything to do with smell and Sight.

The store would be empty of misfits celebrating Christmas for the first time this year. But it would be ready. Yes, ready...for the others.

William planned on staying out at the ranch over Christmas. Timmon frowned, then relaxed. No problem. William and Emma would need to stand together to handle the recriminations of the Mafia sisters and whoever showed up at the store.

He was happy to stay at the desert store and keep an eye on the buzzards that were beginning to collect. They would be here soon. He strode to the phone to call William. When William answered, he said simply, "Hurry up."

Silence may be empty and full of answers,
but you know, I've always been a prancer
a filly takin' plenty a' chances.
Hell, I've had songs written about me
an' my love of red roses.

Part Two

Susan Sugar Diamond.

Red Roses
Roses may be up to 35 million years old, with complex family trees and over 30 thousand varieties worldwide. But the red rose we are referring to was first planted in 1867 in a little town called Bentryille.

When you walk up to my front door, I mean for you to catch on quick and easy to what the snow-white door and the huge wreath adorning it means. It means I have a big Nature I intend to obey. I am a wild and free and blossoming wreath, a never-ending circle blowing in the trade winds that help my earthy Nature soar. My soul won't be caught and held by anyone or anything for long. No, not for long. No one's can, but most other folks don't seem to know that, and they live in bondage willingly. I don't. And I won't.

The only thing that ever shuts me up when I get started good are the red roses blooming in the hothouse as pure white snow slowly collects on the ground in the atrium in my mansion. I watch for silent hours through the windows, fascinated. Once upon a time, I was a tiny red rose that got laid down in the snow in front of an orphanage door. I suspect my mother and father were red roses, too, but I never found them.

Susan Sugar Diamond. That's me. And proud of it. I smile and laugh my hearty big laugh, and you got the best you'll ever get. My front door is huge, and no, it's not two doors, just one giant one. Oversized and curvy, like me. Like something a gnome or a troll would choose. I keep the door painted Snow White—you know why? If you don't, figure it out—kiss kiss. I hang a giant wreath on it year-round. It is a circle telling others not to try to figure me out. There's no beginning and end to me. Actually, that's a damn hopeful thing for anyone, isn't it?

A wreath of almost too tall brilliant red poppies twisted into long, wild meadow grass. They lounge together on the wreath, as though regimentation would never dare come near them. No short little stubby stems all the same size. No good, nice little posies all standing in a row, ruffled, standing exactly where they should, demure behind a plastic bow or some stupid, goofy glitter.

A handful of orange and yellow poppies always mixed in for good measure, just to let the observer know that behind that snow-white, huge curved door lives a soul with unexpected answers and amazing aspects. The wreath looks carelessly thrown together, but trust me, it isn't. It was damn hard work to bring the wild Nature I own into a reflection on the wreath.

My house is all white inside, too. Another sign of who I am. My front door opens onto red flooring, the red of the Eucharist, the born again. Buttery soft, white leather sofas and chairs dot the large interior landscape of my living room here and there, like vast polar bears lazing in a red floored arctic landscape. Red vases full of tall spears of snow-white flowers repose on tables and in nooks. It is easy to like red and white. Two simple colors. Two vibrations of purity and courage. White for purity and red for the ballsiness of the Earth warrior. For me, red is the color of courage plus dashing insouciance. I have both. Always did.

Glass walls circle the atrium in the center of my house. Inside the atrium, splashes of red and white flowers intermix with green foliage with snow sometimes falling on them. You ask, how can snow fall in the summertime? Well, there is no summertime here, except when I want it to be. I am rich enough to stay in snow year-round if I damn well want to. It may look like a careless richness, but I know what I'm doing. Flutes play. Classical music, piano, harps, octaves of dignity wrapping themselves around me. I am a busty, bodacious, compact blond with a head of hair a mammoth would envy. I look like a throwback to all those curvy, lusty, big breasted cavewomen in Bad B movies.

Yep. That's me. Yep, I am Miss Susan Sugar Diamond. Yep, I am a famous author, read by millions all over the world. My Christmas tearjerkers have become the yearly staple of the Hollywood movies. The ones I write in-between don't do so bad, either. Yep, I stay very private. I'm actually a shy star. An old lady now. You laugh. Don't. There are more of us around than you think. Toughies. I just know how to tune myself and my audience so that we reach the same conclusions on the same levels of our being. Sounds haughty. It isn't. Just calibrated synchronicity.

I'm a legendary recluse these days. One who has developed inner resources—albeit unknown to others—since I got older. I was headed this way all along. It just took me years to shut up and think about life instead of mouthing off about it. My life is still my business, though I give others the necessary glimpses to keep them happy and buying my books.

There are two things you don't know about me. The first is that I'm terribly lonely. All orphans are. It's a core level emotional issue when you have no parents from the start. That being said, I think the most difficult thing in the world is trying to be somebody you're not. Usually, you learn who you are from dear old mom and dad and your relatives. Also from your environment. You don't question it. You take it for granted. Unless you grew up without any of those things. Then you get to create yourself, if you've got the guts, the balls to do it. I did. I always owned a big mouth—with plenty to say. I learned the hard way to shut up. But each time I shut up, all those pent up words built up inside me.

A time finally came when I was forced to do something with them or burst, so I began writing instead of talking so much. Talking always got me in trouble anyway, like it did Mae West, who I resemble. Writing got me big bucks, and no one else could make me mind them again. Or make me shut up. Such are the pleasures of having big money, like one of my favorite authors, Esme Emerald Dayton (one of my pen names) who I meet for lunch once in a while to discuss the mysteries she writes.

I write like crazy because I am old, and I started writing the good stuff almost too late in my life for it to do any good. Lana says, not. She says I just think that because I am an old soul. I never could imagine doing anything else once I got started writing. That has kept me at it. I can't write any differently than I do. It's all I am. It's all I have. I don't give away secrets easily. Never. I am a secret. I started out as a secret, a living breathing secret, a secret my parents hid, whoever they were. That is my biggest secret. That I am a secret. Pretty damn well kept, because I never did find them. Evidently, mumsy and daddy were excellent secret keepers too.

I haven't found a cure for any diseases or led people to a better place. I'm just a writer. I never stop writing. At least in my head. It's just that some days I don't put pen to paper. We all fail at things. Such is life. But I struggle past whatever it is and keep on going, hoping that someday someone will see me and hold out their hand and pull me to a safe harbor.

About that old soul thing Lana insists on...Oh, I'm sure I would have loved my mother. Maybe even my father. Definitely any siblings. Aunts, uncles, cousins, grannies, whatever. But someone must have known what my nature was going to be, so they gave me all the freedom that goes with never having a family. I have to say that both sides must have their ups and downs.

I'm sure Miss Charlotte Olivia Masters, head of the orphanage, knew who my mother and father were because she went against her nature by protecting me and encouraging Lana and Serena to befriend me. Miss Charlotte Olivia Master's going against her nature always required lots of money. Well, she's deader than a doornail now, and there are no records, so I guess I'll never know.

I'm a tough, badass lady, who was forced to hurry around the block because of being a blond and because of people assuming I'm a dumbass from growing up in an orphanage. I was forced to confront, confront, confront, every damn day of my life to keep my tits intact (unfondled), and my ass in my britches. Not to mention that my full lips gave the word collagen new meaning. Still do, though I have matured into an older woman. So much for Lana's soul plane theory. I'm not your tame little house cat. I'm a jaguar. I have never been forced to enhance any of me with any product, but I wouldn't hesitate to do so if needed.

Yes, I'm all natural, except for a few necessary effects here and there, and I'm damn tough. When you see me, don't get the idea that I'm not as strong as I need to be. Try me, and you'll find out. I'm no blowhard. I have bodyguards stationed in places you can't see. I learned while I was enrolled in the School of Hard Knocks to think larger and bigger and easier in my mind if I was to ever overcome anything.

It took time to develop the famous, big, hearty laugh that makes people smile. I did it by standing in front of a mirror, practicing for countless hours. And my famous walk. The long-legged, confident stride that a short person rarely accomplishes took walls lined with mirrors in a huge private room with a high ceiling, instructors, and months of practice. I stay ruthless in a sunny way. I try to keep it going smooth, but when needed, I can turn into your worst, big-mouthed badass. Don't push me. I'm a quick learner. I advertise that fact way ahead of time.

Still, sometimes I need to get away from it all and rest and renew myself. That's when I move to my house by the ocean where I can listen to the water roaring night and day until it drives me so crazy I have to leave and retreat back into the silence of snow. The snow blanket calms my adrenals back down again. The red roses build my courage up once again.

My books sell like hotcakes. People can't wait to read them. My best sellers are my Christmas novels. They are stories about orphaned children finding new homes or growing up alone as pure, sweet, self-sacrificing orphans, at last finding a nice family and true love. I write them, drawing from my own experience at the orphanage, adding one piece of the awfulness I survived in that place to each story, then working out a positive ending for it. I'm thinking I'll never run out of stories.

I re-named myself Susan Sugar Diamond when I was seven. I was a foundling at the beginning of my life, given a name you wouldn't recognize—a plain-Jane name, but I was different than the others. My new name made it easier for me to survive in a world full of dull gray clones. I fluffed up my beauty and made the most of it.

Here's the real deal.

Many orphanages are small, though people don't realize it. Most people are used to industrial-sized everything. They tend to think of orphanages as large institutions, like hospitals or something.

Miss Charlotte Olivia Masters Home for Orphans was located down at the end of Tenth Street, on the south edge of small-town Bentryville. Beyond it lay fields and trees and farms.

The orphanage was quickly launched by Miss Charlene Olivia Masters because of her brother, a deacon in the Methodist Church. The vain and handsome Mr. Troubadour Jake Masters began leading any number of females in town astray from the time he reached puberty, carelessly leaving the fruit of his loins behind for them to raise. No one dared complain because his family ran the town. His philandering ways continued until one finally came back to haunt him, forcing him to quickly mend his ways with the help of his astute wife and spinster sister.

His big mistake was the wife of a Bible salesman traveling through town. Proud and haughty Mr. Troubadour Jake Masters, whose family founded the town and still owned half of it, met the young wife in the back of the empty church on a Wednesday night while her Bible salesman husband looked the other way. Armed with a gift of cash, the couple hurried out of town just before dawn, while Mr. Troubadour Jake Masters went home to join his proud and haughty wife in bed, sated, satisfied that he would see no more of them.

But much to his surprise, about a year later, when he'd forgotten all about the juicy young wife and the Bible salesman, their gift to him was placed on his doorstep in a basket, squalling its guts out.

The doorbell rang in the middle of the night. Mr. Troubadour Jake Masters haughty wife, Mrs. Elvira Mason Masters, hurried downstairs to answer it. She opened the door to find a lusty, squalling baby laying in a basket on her doorstep, arms flailing angrily.

She hastily grabbed up the basket and carried it inside, closing the door quickly behind her. She hoped the neighbors didn't see anything. Mrs. Elvira Mason Masters, president of the garden society and leading social club member, looked closely at the baby. It was about three months old, and every part of it looked exactly like Mr. Troubadour Jake Masters, right down to the cleft in its chin and its webbed first and second toe.

Mr. Troubadour Jake Masters swiftly did the figures and confessed his misdeed to his wife.

"T'was the Bible salesman's wife. She led me on. Forced herself on me, she did."

Mrs. Elvira Mason Masters didn't believe a word her husband said. He was a philanderer, always was and always would be. She knew it when she married him. But she liked being the wife of one of the most prominent citizens in Bentryville. There were many perks in it for a former pork farmer's daughter. She'd kept quiet and given the matter of his philandering ways much deep thought over the years, and she'd made a plan to be carried out if worst ever came to worst. And here it was.

Mrs. Elvira Mason Masters carried the lusty, screaming child up to Miss Charlotte Olivia Master's bedroom, shoved open the door, and presented the baby to her. Miss Charlotte Olivia Masters, whiny old maid and permanent guest in her brother's home, not to mention a big thorn in his wife's side, could raise her brother's child. If her luck held, Mrs. Elvira Mason Masters would get rid of both the baby and Miss Charlotte Olivia Masters.

Word spread like wildfire as it does through any small town. The almost finished red brick building the prosperous Mr. Troubadour Jake Masters was having built on the edge of town was no longer going to be a bicycle factory. The building stopped, and it was suddenly turned over to his only sister, Miss Charlotte Olivia Masters, who quickly went to work spreading good deeds all around the little town of Bentryville.

"My generous brother has deeded the building to me, and it's going to be an orphanage," Miss Charlotte Olivia Masters said, lifting her eyes heavenward. "God's work will be done through taking care of homeless children."

The lusty baby boy, who stubbornly remained the spitting image of Mr. Troubador Jake Masters, was bundled off to the Miss Charlotte Olivia Master's Home for Orphans as soon as she moved in, which happened before the paint dried on the walls.

Snow was falling thick and steady on Christmas Eve around midnight when whoever it was that did the dastardly deed laid their blanket wrapped love child down in front of the huge double doors at the front of the orphanage.

I've pictured the scene many times. A dark night filled with falling snow, the red brick orphanage standing solid and staid on the edge of the quaint little town of Bentryville, two golden lights glowing in their black sconces on each side of huge, polished wood doors, voices singing past those doors. It was almost time for the midnight Christmas caroling signifying the birth of Christ when I was laid down outside the orphanage doors. I guess I was to be their holy child.

The choir had just stopped singing, and Miss Charlotte Olivia Masters and the staff were readying themselves for the yearly Christmas sermon given by Mr. Troubadour Jake Masters. I screamed during that fateful lull, which is why I ended up inside the orphanage instead of freezing to death outside. A frozen holy child. Not too smart, Mom and Dad. Why the hell my parents didn't knock on the door is beyond me. Dunces! I screamed many times. Loudly, to make sure I was rescued. I was a strong and lusty, full of life baby, and I sure as hell didn't intend on ending up as a frozen lollipop because of stupid parents.

I was dumped in front of the doors to Miss Charlotte Olivia Master's Home for Orphans dressed in a gorgeous red and white outfit, shoes, coat, and a bonnet, wrapped in a terrifyingly expensive blanket—the best money could buy. My friend Lana said the rich folks dumped their "mistakes" at the orphanage and gave regular secret donations to the orphanage to keep their "mistakes" taken care of. That's what kept the orphanage in business. Fortunately for me, I was a screamer, and I screamed just at the right time. I can still scream loud enough to wake the dead.

Growing up in the orphanage, I liked to daydream that I was left in front of a sweet, little old lonely granny's cottage, a granny who needed a companion and asked for one for Christmas. Or, I was left at the door of a fun-loving family who'd yearned for a baby almost into old age but couldn't have one, or I was left at the door of a mansion whose butler discovered me and carried me inside to his kindly mistress who was wasting away with nothing to live for, like in those fake, famous child actress movies. I wished any of those other crap stories were true, but no, it was a home for shady ladies and men's offspring I was dumped in front of.

No doubt I was dumped in front of the Miss Charlotte Olivia Master's Home for Orphans by a gorgeous, loving mother with a scarf tied close around her honey-colored curls to tame them, and an extremely handsome, dimpled chinned father who held rumbles of laughter in his manly chest.

I knew this was true because I was beautiful. I never once looked like a skinny, little ugly varmint. Not even for one second. I knew better, even before I was out of the cradle, or should I say the crib they put me in. My smiles and cooing got me the best of everything the orphanage had to offer. Which wasn't much. No diarrhea or spitting up for me. No crass wailing for a diaper change. I peed and crapped just before someone showed up to check on our "diedies," their nickname for diapers. I walked quickly, to hell with crawling.

Serena was my best friend in the orphanage. She was close to my only other friend Lana's age. Both of them looked out for me. You see, my cuteness could have got me in all kinds of trouble, for people came to adopt kids for different reasons. Back then, they were mostly honest about their reasons for adopting. Usually, they simply wanted a homely child to use as a free servant. Someone to work for them. Some nameless kid who didn't matter. No one ever checked to find out if they were good or bad parents. They just shoved the kid out the door, glad to have another one gone, making room for yet another unwanted offspring, usually the result of fornication and secret lusts.

The orphanage was safe because of Serena and Lana. It was my only home. The only one I knew, and I didn't want to leave it. Serena taught me how to stay, how to never get chosen, though I was beautiful. She taught me the art of drooling and shuffling and doing things in slow motion with a blank look on my face when the adopters came around. Serena was a little bit that way naturally. So, we both got to grow up in Miss Charlotte Olivia Masters Home for Orphans. That's why when I got rich, I looked her up. She was living in a home for the destitute and handicapped. I got her out of that dismal place and moved her into one of the guesthouses on my property. I hired people to help her because she was much worse with her walking and memory over the years from neglect. She has her own staff who meet her needs, and she has the best of everything. No problem. She walks with her head held high now and wears lovely long removable collars around her neck instead of an obvious bib to catch any accidental drooling.

Though her memory is mostly gone, she knows she has no money worries to make her worsen quicker. That makes all the difference in the world. I hired a companion for her, for I am too busy to sit with her and don't want to. She doesn't seem to need that from me anyway, just the services.

Lana and Serena were my two "sisters" at the orphanage. Lana cut my hair and sewed clothes for me, smiled into my eyes, and saw me. She named me Susan Sugar and left it at that. I picked up Diamond, after Lincoln Diamond, who came along later. Lana re-named herself Lana Ellis when she was eight. She refused to accept the name Smith, which was given to all us orphans as a last name. She won, too. She eavesdropped in on Miss Charlotte Olivia Master's phone calls, then dropped by the Mayor's office for a visit, and that was it. When I was dumped at the orphanage, Lana Ellis was already a badass ten-year-old kid who didn't give in under threats of death, shame, or ridicule.

Lana put up with my random silliness and constant reading. She knew my secrets. She knew how much I loved watching the one skimpy tree at the back of the yard get its leaves. When it started budding out again, my hopes grew along with it. Elated, I stared through the window or sneaked out back in the cold spring winds and leaned up against the wall to the side of the back porch where no one could see me.

Everything we loved or became attached to was taken away from us by the other orphans. They destroyed it or took it for themselves. The game they liked most was to watch us cry while they destroyed something of ours. Wisely, like the rest, I hid my likes and loves and left them hidden to grow inside as they would.

"Someday, I will have all the things I want, and no one will take them away from me!" I thought grimly.

"Someday, I'll be out of here, and I will do whatever I want. I will love whoever I please and like whatever I want to."

The older kids took our food away from us. They set us to fighting with each other. We wore their hand-me-downs. However, it wasn't so bad for me. There were a handful of us that Miss Charlotte Olivia Masters wouldn't let the others go too far with. No nosebleeds or beatings while her back was turned. No slipping around in the night. If the rest bothered us, she simply locked them in a closet for a day or three. No food, no water, no place to piss. And they cleaned the "punishment" closet as soon as she let them out, or back in they went.

There were three of us under her silent, unspoken—I have no doubt—well-paid protection. Finally, I came to understand that I was getting special treatment. Who were my fairy godparents? I went straight to Miss Charlotte Olivia Master's study one day to find out. I opened the door and walked in. She was sitting at her desk, writing. She glared at me with a scowl as I advanced down the long room towards her.

"What do you want?" she asked curtly.

"Who are my fairy godparents?" I asked. Being the ripe old age of six should have made my question real cute instead of stupid. But she didn't smile.

"What do you mean?" she asked.

"Well, somebody takes care of me. Somebody pays you money to keep me okay. That's what the older kids say. Who's my mama and daddy?"

I said this without any expectation of trouble, but it came fast.

"Those liars! You'll never know, you little brat! Nobody knows! Don't you ever come in here again without my permission!"

She jumped up out of her chair, rushed around her desk and grabbed me by the arm. She ran with me to the door, shoved me through it, and slammed it shut behind me. My arm hurt. I looked at it. She'd bruised it. Nursing my grievance, I went off to find Serena and Lana. Maybe they knew what was going on. But they didn't have any answers, just comfort to offer.

That winter, I watched the snow falling through the windows for hours. It snowed heavily during the long winter months in Bentryville. I traced circles on the window panes and wondered how many kinds of snow there were. I wondered if the snow slanted sideways when it blew over the highway heading out of Bentryville. Did snowflakes thin down as they floated to Earth through the atmosphere, or did they pick up weight and grow larger? The snow came and covered everything with cold white like I was almost covered as a baby before my loud-mouthed rescue. I came to love snow. I wondered if my parents were dead. But I knew, even back then, that I was better off wondering about snow than wondering who my parents were, and why they'd abandoned me as a baby. Wondering about that was an exercise in futility.

Serena was a decade older than me, like Lana. She couldn't read well, but oh, she could cook! Lana worked in the kitchen too, and her chicken and dumplings were beyond compare. They let me eat what I needed while the others at the everlasting, charming Miss Charlotte Olivia Master's Home for Orphans in the small town of Bentryville complained about their portions.

There were three floors in the orphanage. The layout was odd because the building was originally intended to be a bicycle manufacturing plant. The first floor was filled with factory sized rooms. Miss Charlotte Olivia Master's parlor, her bedroom, her bathroom, a kitchen in the back, and the huge all-purpose room we orphans ate in, studied in, and played in. Staff rooms were on the second floor. Our rows of beds were up on the third-floor attic. A guard was posted each night to make sure we didn't wander out of our beds and down the stairs into places we weren't supposed to be. Like the kitchen.

There was a swing set and a sandbox out back in the big yard. We spent summers out there, fighting over the swings and the little bit of sand in the sandbox. The gate was locked, and they watched us so we didn't climb over the fence and run away.

The town of Bentryville couldn't ignore our existence, though they tried. We were the living heirs of the town's sins. Mr. Troubadour Jake Masters kept on with his philandering ways. In fact, he and some others became bolder because there was now a convenient place for the women who got "caught" to unload their "mistakes."

Miss Charlotte Olivia Masters, with her brother's backing, kept the town up to date on their sins by making us dutifully attend church Sunday mornings. If the town had to keep their mouths shut about their own philandering and its results, then they knew to keep them shut about Mr. Troubadour Jake Masters philandering, and he knew it. We attended the Methodist Church one week, a different church the next. No church in town or its occupants were beneath our attendance. We were a weekly reminder of their sins.

Wherever we attended, we were vigorously ignored by the churchgoers. I studied the attendees of the various churches. After a while, I realized it was true. Some of the inhabitants of the orphanage looked just like some of the church people. The orphans older than me already knew who belonged to whom. A few of them were openly favored by certain townspeople for being "smart" or "a go-getter" or for "their singing voices." They discreetly received packages or were escorted to the park for afternoon visits with what Miss Charlotte Olivia Masters termed "interviews with prospective adopters."

I searched the churches every Sunday with an eye out for my mother and father while the preachers droned on, but I never saw anyone my equal in blond-haired, blue-eyed Kewpie doll beauty.

Bless whoever it was that gifted me with a ferocious imagination, for it blossomed the first time I sat down to write. I wasn't called to write anything. I never had an inkling or inclination to write. Nothing driving me. Absolutely nothing. All I wanted to do was complain about the goddamned orphanage. Feeling like a wimpy victim, I sat down and started writing my grievances out on a couple sheets of paper. I ran out of paper. Caught short, pacing and breathing heavily with outrage, I knew it wasn't enough. There was more to say. Maybe plenty. Maybe I should write my life story. Vent, get it out of my system. That would require more than two pieces of paper. Inspiration struck me. I could buy a journal. I could write everything down in a journal. I rushed out and bought three journals and a pile of loose paper. Three because I felt my insides expanding into more. The stopper had just been pulled out of the bottle, so to speak.

Pen on paper was too slow for my thoughts and emotions. Journaling was too slow, too personal. I wanted to shout my misery from the rooftops. I bought a typewriter down at Gamble's Hardware and General Store, toted it home and began using the stacks of blank paper. I loved the crisp clacks of each letter. Lana urged me to take typing in high school and I did. She said I would make a secretary no one would forget, if nothing else. And with my looks, I could end up marrying the boss. That was her plan for me. Not mine. Mine was to have money without marrying the boss in an era of time when men ran the show even more than they do now.

The words poured swiftly out onto clean white sheets of paper. They looked like white sheets dancing in the wind, the black letters on each page fading in the sunlight or dancing off in the wind like when it stirred clean sheets to flapping. I lost track of time. I wrote and went hungry and didn't bathe and didn't go out. I went without sleep and other's voices. A stack of neatly typed sheets became two, then three.

After a few days, when I didn't show up anywhere, I heard Lana pounding on my door. I wouldn't answer until she shouted that she was going to call the cops to break in and see if I was dead. I jumped to my feet and rushed the door. I jerked it open and glared at her. She took a step back.

"Phew! You stink! What the hell's been going on here? Anybody else in the house?"

"No!" I shouted at her. "Now leave me alone! I'm busy."

I tried to shut the door in her face, but she shoved her way past me. I glared at her, hands on my hips.

"What the hell are you doing?" she asked as she eyed the typewriter, the neat stacks of paper, the tumbled pillows and half-eaten junk food scattered around the typewriter. Crumpled papers were tossed everywhere, and the smells of sweat and old garbage filled the air. But near a window, on a small shiny table with nothing else on it, lay three neat stacks of pages. Lana zeroed in on them.

"What's that?" she asked, heading toward them. She grabbed the stack of papers. I watched her stride to the sofa, sweep aside the junk piled on it, and sit down. She started reading. A feeling of gratification filled me. Though I didn't know it at the time, she was reading my first book. After a while, she said, "Clean up this mess while I read." I was empty and happy. I'd just finished the last page when she knocked, anyway. I cleaned up the place and showered. I was thirty-five.

÷

Back in the orphanage, when I turned twelve, a boy kept hitting my large, newly forming breasts. A girl named Trudy was insanely jealous of me, and she put him up to it. I made a plan. There was just so much I would take off of anybody, and the twelve-year-old boy and spiteful Trudy were not going to bring me down. Someday, somebody might. But he'd have to be a hell of a man.

One day, I calmly cut the top of the boy's head open with a butter knife I'd stolen from the kitchen. I cut lightly, and only for an inch or two. While he bled, I told him very calmly that I would kill him if he punched my chest again. I spoke softly, but I damn well meant it, and he knew it. He fell to the floor like

I'd already killed him. Damn ham! One-upped me that time.

Everybody came running. I glared at Trudy, edged up to her, and whispered, "You're next, bitch." There was more trouble out of her, but not for a while. Evil like that has to recuperate each time it is dealt a blow. But it always comes back. Sooner or later.

When "Mother" Charlotte Olivia Masters and the latest "Father" Smith got home, they glared at me with such hate and fury that I never remembered their words. I've never forgotten the looks on their faces. I told them the boy kept punching me in the chest with his fists and I intended to live to grow up, and I wasn't going to put up with any kind of chest problems because of his sorry ass. Trudy and the boy wanted them to throw me out. They tried to scare me and they threatened me, but inside I knew they were cowards and wouldn't stand up to me for long because I had the right of it.

Shortly after that incident, Mother Masters decided to hire the family Poorvis as caretakers. They moved into the back rooms of the orphanage along with their big brood of lazy, mean, noisy, dumb kids. I called them the Poser family behind their backs because they sure knew how to fake out both the government and "Mother" Charlotte Olivia Masters. Mr. Poorvis was supposed to be a handyman and a jack of all trades. He was to mow the lawns and fix everything, clean the basement, and so forth.

Mrs. Poorvis was to clean and cook and babysit us. Instead, they laid around and complained and ate. The staff joined right in with them, and soon nothing got done around the place. The orphans were assigned to do the work.

The Poorvis family included their fat son named Dorr. Dorr Hellman Poorvis was a bully. No matter what he did, the Poorvis parents defended him and hid it from everyone while he whined and hid behind closed doors and they carried food and comforting words to him. I dreamed of poisoning him and killing him off a thousand different ways each night.

Then there was Dirk, the other Poorvis son. He wandered around in an alcoholic fog, seeing things and having chats with them and tying up kids and locking them in closets and in trunks.

Suffice it to say that it was a nerve-wracking, testy time for us kids living in the orphanage while being forced to partake of the generous government hospitality paid monthly to the place. The orphanage was cold in the winter, and we quickly learned to stay outdoors in the spring, summer, and fall. Food was scarce because Mr. Poorvis drank much of the government budget up. When the ladies of the town brought us the usual Christmas presents and favors, the Poorvis family took them as their own. In school, the kids began calling us the "Pooraspiss Kids," or the Poopandpiss Kids." It was a big step down.

Where was "Mother" Charlotte Olivia Masters during all this? She maintained her own "apartment" in the orphanage, but spent most of her time traveling with the latest "Mr. Smith or Jones."

After I became a successful author, I checked out Trudy Smith to see what happened to her. Hopefully, I pictured her as a slattern with a bunch of whining, dirty kids hanging on to her worn out apron while she fried up government portions of meat in a dirty, smelly, hot kitchen. I wasn't far off the mark. She became the headmistress of a private school for girls and was later let go and chastised for cruelty. She married hastily to a tailor and reared a bunch of mean kids. Trudy Smith became the Christmas villain in a large number of my Christmas books.

I went back to the orphanage just once to find out if I missed out on anything. Maybe my mother left a letter for me, and it was still there. After all, the Divine, or karma or whatever you call spirit, sent me to live there for some reason. I just wanted to know what the reason or reasons were.

"James, let's go to the orphanage." James sighed and nodded reluctantly. He had very persuasive methods of getting across what he was thinking without using words.

"Are you sure?" he asked. "Yes," I nodded firmly.

We got on the road. A few days later, James drew to a stop at the curb. I stared at the orphanage. The fence was rusty and broken. The metal gate hung crooked, squeaking in the wind. The yard was high with unkempt grass that needed mowing. The orphanage was painted flat shades of ugly gray now. The paint was peeling, showing old red brick in places. Weeds shoved their victorious way up through cracks in the wide, crumbling sidewalk.

I applied fresh, fire engine red lipstick and fluffed the shoulders of my white ostrich feather wraparound before I stepped out of the car. I started up the sidewalk and glanced back at James, my chauffeur, waiting for me in my latest acquired land yacht, a red and white 1959 Pontiac Bonneville with red leather interior. I hate driving any place when I can ride. He frowned at me and shook his head.

"Don't do it, Miss!" he called after me. I grinned pertly at him.

I rang the doorbell and waited. After a long time, I heard a shuffling sound. The front door or the orphanage groaned and scraped open and I found myself staring into the face of "Father" Poorvis. He looked like hell. Bad. As in sick. His hair was greasy, and he was dirty and unshaven. I could smell him from where I stood.

"Father Poorvis?"

"What do you want? We're not buying anything. Even if you do look like a hooker."

He leered at me. I took an involuntary step back.

"It's Susan. Remember me?"

He looked me up and down.

"Well, well, well. We thought we'd seen the last of you."

He held the door open for me. I followed him into the living room.

"Set down," he said.

I perched gingerly on the edge of a worn-out sofa close to the front door. The place was appalling. Dusty and grime with dogs and cats everywhere. Mr.

Poorvis noticed me looking around. No kids, though. I figured there would be a passel of offspring from the loins of at least Dorr and his brother lying around the place, puking and whining like their fathers.

"Not the way we used to keep it for the government. We don't get orphans anymore. Not for a long time. Everybody else is gone. A long time ago."

He sat back in his chair and studied me with greedy little pig eyes. Just then, "Mother" Poorvis stepped out of the kitchen, wiping her hands on a worn-out dish towel. She glared at me suspiciously. Without taking her eyes off me, she spoke to Mr. Poorvis.

"What are you doing, letting people in here?"

"This ain't people. This is Susan."

"Mother" Poorvis glared at me. Then she looked me over, and I saw a gleam of speculation spark in her eyes.

"Susan," she said. I nodded. "Well, you're looking....good. Looks like life has been treating you well."

I nodded. I could barely speak for the shock and horror I was feeling. Why did I come here?

"Well, that's more than I can say for us!"

"Mother" Poorvis rushed an old chair at the end of the dingy sofa and sat down. She began wringing her hands together.

"Dorr is in prison. A lot of people had it in for him, even though he's just an innocent boy."

She sneaked a calculating look at me to gauge how I was taking her words. I nodded in fake, mournful sympathy, while my innards roared with the practical suggestion, "Get the hell out of here!" This was a huge mistake! I was terrified of what they might think up to do to me. Then I remembered James was out in the car, and I calmed down a little bit.

"Dirk is in a sanitarium. Them liars say he is mentally unbalanced. They wouldn't let us have any more orphans after Dorr got one in trouble. You know what I mean."

Father Poorvis leered at me. I looked away.

"We just stay broke and hard up all the time," Mother Poorvis said mournfully. She poured out a long litany of their troubles while I sat frozen to the sofa. After what seemed like forever, she gestured around the room.

"See how it is now?" She smirked at me craftily. "Well, it looks like you've been doing okay. It looks like you got a lot more than us, and we could sure use some help from you. After all, we give you a good home."

She shrugged.

"You owe us. We helped raise you."

I'd had enough. I do have a temper in spite of my fear. I jumped up and rushed the front door and jerked it open. My legs were shaking.

"No. You didn't. I raised myself."

I stepped out and slammed the door shut behind me. I raced down the steps in high heels, fleeing the gray and broken pieces of the orphanage and the Poorvis part of my life. I wanted to leave them behind forever. Now I could. And would. If I came up with any more unanswered questions, I would hire a detective to find the answers. I ran down the sidewalk toward James. He was leaning up against the passenger side of the car, waiting for me. He ran forward, grabbed me, and led me to the car. The front door of the orphanage opened. I heard them shouting.

"You whore! Won't help us after we raised you!"

I whirled around and glared at them. The last little bit of secret hope I'd nurtured, telling myself that maybe I'd read it wrong during the years I lived in "Monster Mansion," that these people once actually cared for me, if only just a little bit when I was a child, fled for the last time.

I stared at what was left of the ugly orphanage, remembering skimpy, bad food, fighting off kids, the constant work, and rage-filled shouts. The Poorvis couple had taken the orphanage from a livable place down into the depths of hardship, despair, and ugliness. There was nothing left of the orphanage I'd known. I was right all along. Now it was confirmed. There was nothing left except bad in this place now, and bad in these people.

James grabbed my shoulders, turned me around, and gently guided me into the car. It took until I was inside sitting on the soft leather seat with the door closed between them and me to regain my composure.

James studied me in the rearview mirror. I stared back at him while I reapplied a coat of fresh red lipstick, then stared out the window at my old home. I tried to picture my parents laying me in front of the orphanage door. I tried to remember the countless times I'd dreamed of them coming to find me, but I drew a blank. That's when I realized those parts of my life were finally over. Hopefully, I could still write Christmas books. Maybe my orphans would start out life in a better place with bigger dreams now.

The place was closed, its windows shuttered—three floors of faded red brick emptiness. The parking lot was empty. James kept the engine idling, as though he couldn't get away fast enough. We watched a page of yellowed newspaper scrape across the ground and get caught on the ragged edge of the rusty metal fence with the faded metal sign with missing letters that once read "Miss Charlotte Olivia Masters Home for Orphans."

"Let's go home," I said to him.

"Yes, Ma'am. Good idea."

I never went back. No need to.

÷

At home, my writing changed. It grew stronger, more versatile. My fingers flew over the typewriter and later, my first keyboard, leaving trails of words in black and white. Words shared from me to those women out there who needed gigantic hugs just as much as I did on their endless foraging for love and companionship throughout life. And so, I continued writing my romance novels, knowing that I would write until I stopped. I put all of the ups and downs and my affairs of the heart and mind and the physical, all of it into them.

I chose one bad thing to write about, a challenge to be overcome for each romance novel. One by one, I wrote about my shames and humiliations and the disgusting, mean things that once happened to me. My heroines always wore an air of naivety and innocence that could not be taken away from them through thick or thin, or through the vilest behaviors of the bad people they encountered.

The place where each heroine's bravery lived became a constant. The courage of an innocent, who wouldn't and couldn't look at what was obviously right in front of her, and it still turned out right. When evil crossed their paths, my heroines hummed and picked flowers and carefully tiptoed away from its seething, deadly presence. They absolutely would not look at it.

I wrote about what I'd seen happen to the other girls and boys in the orphanage. Most came and went fairly quickly. It was easy to find out what happened to some of them, for they were usually taken in by local families or families living fairly close to the orphanage. Others were gone for good—out of sight, but never out of my recall. I wondered what happened to them and in later years, hired someone to find the kids that were in the orphanage with me, however briefly. Most of them had been worked into the ground and given little or no education. They were living mean little lives with husbands or wives like themselves, raising a bunch of kids. They'd been used as free labor.

If they needed help, I gave it anonymously. I did it because they had no parents either. No one to stand up for them. No one to love them in those most important ways.

Although Serena and Lana once protected me to a great degree from the brutality around us in the orphanage, the three of us didn't have what we needed to go forth and live the kind of storybook life we hoped for or envisioned. So I lent a hand. A few of the orphans had anonymous parents back in the orphanage days who contributed to their well being. I became one too, without any issue from my loin's involvement, if you get my drift.

Other than writing smarmy Christmas stories, which is probably my unconscious crying out (plaintively, of course) for mummy and daddy to come and take me home each year at Christmas instead of leaving me laying in the snow at the front door of a lousy orphanage—without knocking—I write about ditzy, naive, women wanting to believe the best. Women needing, wanting to fall in love with a love that companions them all their life. I write about lonely, lovely hearts searching through the dark alleys and endless nights of life, lonely hearts hidden behind dull, menial jobs, lonely women who are mute to their children. Lives lived with half loves and not much fun. Then some kind of miracle occurs like it did for me, and they are set free into a good life.

I was set free into money and a good life with my first book. I made buckets of money. I never had any money to speak of before, so I went nuts with it. Being an orphan, I didn't have a clue about money, so it just made it worse. There are no rich orphanages catering to the children passing through on their way to adulthood.

After I came to my senses, I observed how people were treating me differently now that I was rich and some of them realized belatedly, that I had brains. At least enough to write books that made vast amounts of money. I hired bodyguards. No more shouts of, "Poontang!" or grabs or pinches. I hired a staff that stood between me and the people I needed or wanted to fend off. I moved out of the small house I'd rented for years and bought a larger one. Eventually, I hired an architectural firm and built my own house and one at the ocean.

I went through a half a dozen men who "loved me," but it was my money they were after. Those relationships hurt, so I learned to take lovers and leave the romance out of it. I became adept at short term relationships with men, but underneath I yearned for a steady, quiet man, a slow-handed lover. I wanted a man with internal steel and the heat that comes from making love for love's sake, not for any other reason.

I got tired of taking lovers a long time ago. I live alone and deliberately isolate, except for my staff. I am plumper now but never lost my figure. I still wear fine clothes, colorful with good tailoring, the same bright red lipstick, and excellent, demure, makeup. I know where to stick "demure." I've known for a long time where it belongs.

It took me a while, though. Red or white and sometimes the turquoise of Miami waters or the cabled salmons of the setting suns over Capri, or the mystic, dark blue swirling colors of the Bering Sea, or the magic greens of Mauna Loa is what I wear. My designers color cloth until they come up with a color I like. I find it delightful to dress in Nature's proud beauty. I like tall boots and good looking, unusual shoes. And books. I own oceans of them. And opera. I have plenty of music, too. Still, I yearn.

Roses bloom in shades
dependin' on what ya' got
up yer' sleeves.
den' there's red cactus
I hear tell
bloomin' in da' desert
fer' when ya' ain't got
nothin' else ta' smell.

Part Three

Lana

Lana was remembering the long-ago day that changed her world. It was a day when she could have gotten herself in worse trouble than she already was. She remembered somehow knowing that nobody would bother her for a little while. This same desert had told her so that long ago afternoon.

The heat shimmering across the hot asphalt of the two-lane desert highway was blinding. She stunk. She was thirsty, close to absolute exhaustion. The kind that once left her vulnerable in the orphanage and at the mercy of the latest father. Her eyes were bruised and swollen, blackened, leaking endless tears of unspent misery. The leakage etched slow, dusty channels down her face, past her broken nose and lumpy mouth. Her whole body ached, she hurt from head to toe, and she knew she had a fever. She fiddled with the air conditioner knob, but it still wasn't working. She sighed and looked out the window at the desert filled with thrumming, waving lines of heat.

She'd been handed a death sentence, but she didn't give a damn about that. She'd beat it. What she knew for certain now was that endings, short or long, drew out epiphanies no other part of life could. Endings had to happen. Endings were valuable, always with a purpose. Who would have known? Now that she knew, all she wanted was an ending that wouldn't leave her beat up or broken again. Just one would do.

The little red car she rode in was stolen. It was a small red classic '53 Austin Healy 100. Mitch took it away from his younger brother and gave it to her when they started living together a month ago. He knew she liked red and classic cars. He didn't give a damn about them, but he knew she did. She didn't find out about him taking the car away from his brother until pieces slipped out in conversations during the short month or so she'd lived with him.

Hot rage filled her gut, giving her the energy to keep going. She drew on it. Men! Their lifelong treatment of her was never-ending, and it looked like it would never stop. From her fatherless beginning to the orphanage "fathers" and the foster homes, all her "fathers," "uncles," and "brothers" were lousy dumbasses. Neanderthals. Thank God she was able to mostly avoid them trying to molest her. Her gut cooled a little. No, when she was younger, they just liked to order her around, call her names, slap, pinch, and hit her.

Off in the distance, she saw a little white building. It was a church that turned into a store and gas station as she got closer.

Men! It was the men that came later, the ones she had to change herself for in order to survive. Her thoughts left any innocence behind as she focused her rage on them. She wove down the dusty highway towards the little desert store that looked like a church with gas pumps out front. She glanced at the gas gage. She was lucky to have found anything out in this godforsaken dust bowl. The store was the only thing she'd seen in the empty desert.

She knew her internal fuel was running out, too. She deliberately let the pain from the beating Mitch had given her pump through her body, amping up the rage she carried. Thin and dehydrated as she was, she knew anger was her friend. It would carry her through to some sort of safety, at least for a while, once again.

In one smooth motion, she slid the car off the blacktop and came to a stop in front of the gas pumps. A teenage girl stood on the store porch doing something. She slowly worked her way out of the car and leaned up against it. Everything she owned hurt. Rage filled her. She was running again. She nodded to herself. Her hand felt heavy. She looked down and realized the gun from the glove box was in her hand.

She staggered to the front of the smart, tiny red car as the man walked slowly toward her, wiping his oily hands on a rag. He was short and stocky with brown hair. She thought about shooting him like she'd shot Mitch. Two well-aimed shots, both to the knees. But she needed the gas tank filled first. She motioned to him to fill it. She swelled with rage and hate for all men as she watched him filling her gas tank. Her hand with the gun came up, and she aimed at him.

Suddenly, she felt the deafening silence of the huge desert surrounding her. It was alive and purposeful. She shuddered and lowered the gun. What the hell was going on? What kind of place was this? Her eyes went to the girl standing on the porch. The girl had stopped what she was doing and was watching her. The girl's eyes held hers, flashing a message to her. It seemed this desert wanted her. There was a place in it that she needed to go to RIGHT NOW, and it was close by. The man's voice chimed in, carrying a lower vibration. The place she needed to go to had something to do with red cactus... the cactus would help her?

She lowered the gun and worked her way back into the car and drove away. Not far down the highway, she swerved off onto a small trail and stopped the car at the bottom of a sandy ridge where the trail ended. She climbed out, holding the gun and lurched across the ridge, sometimes whimpering in pain. She stood on the other side, weaving in shocked disbelief. She started laughing out of a corner of her hurt mouth. In front of her stood a row of six wood, red-painted, faded cacti in buckets, propped up by two by fours. A couple of the cactus had doubled up fists. They were all riddled with bullet holes.

She couldn't keep back a painful, lurching laugh. She watched the red cactus brighten. *This was crazy*, she thought. She hee heed again, holding her mouth muscles rigid with her hand. So much easier on her mouth. The cactus brightened a tiny bit more.

She studied them. Why were they there? The answer came to her like a speeding bullet. Evidently, somebody used them to work off their frustrations and doing that made the crazy things happy. Well, there was no time like the present. She raised the gun and shot the cactus in what would be their gonads and knees as if they were human. She shot until the gun was empty.

The desert's purposeful silence settled a mantle of quiet over her. She studied the red cactus again. They were bright and beautiful and actually seemed happy now. After she'd shot them all to pieces. They looked like new and all of them were smiling. Now, that was odd. She shook her head in puzzlement. Could it be that some things or places liked or needed anger, rage, hate, all of that bad stuff? Needed unfairness, never-ending contrariness and weariness? Needed shouting, misery, and grudge-holding? She knew plenty about every one of those things. It was hard for her to stay beautiful with those awful things surrounding her. How come the cactus became more beautiful after being worked over? She studied them again. They wore red, just like her. She'd read somewhere—she loved to read—that red was the color of courage. Well, maybe it was.

The calm of centuries of warriors filled her. Road warriors. Suddenly, she knew she was standing in the sacred place she'd always needed. She was standing on sacred ground, surrounded by warriors like herself. She felt included somewhere at last. She sensed that life had beat the hell out of all the others who'd came here, too. A weird kind of peace filled her.

She turned away, crossed the ridge, got back in the little red car. She stashed the empty gun in the glove box. She made a U-turn and drove out onto the highway, heading in the opposite direction of the store. She fled north, remembering Teddy and Susan.

Susan was out there somewhere and she would find her someday. Not now, but someday. As soon as she was back on her feet again. Susan would lead her to Teddy. Theodore Smith. Love flooded her soul, strengthening her as she drove north. Teddy was the one male human being she loved and would forever. Teddy Smith, the name given to him by their "Mother," Miss Charlotte Olivia Masters, at the orphanage they grew up in.

She'd taken the sickly, pale baby from "Mother" and hurried away with him. He was about three months old when someone dumped him on the front porch of the orphanage. Whoever it was, knocked loud enough to wake the dead, then disappeared. She made it to the door first, wanting to believe, determined to believe that someone was delivering a birthday gift just for her. The orphans in Miss Charlotte Olivia Master's orphanage didn't get birthday presents. Or cake or ice cream. Just a skimpy dinner, as usual. Birthdays were whispered about. Each orphan's birthday was listed in Miss Charlotte's big black Bible as being the date they were found outside the orphanage doors.

Most of the foundlings were adopted into families by the time they were four and could work. The same families "adopted" up to five of the children—foundlings—before the law stopped them. Some of the "foundlings" didn't need to worry. They knew, and Miss Charlotte Olivia Masters knew there was a select group of "foundlings" that would never get adopted out. They grew up in the orphanage while a secret someone paid their way. Some of those orphans figured out that they were products of the loins of the town gentry and strutted around, lording it over the others.

Lana decided Teddy was her birthday gift. She needed him as much as he needed her. She kept him alive with help from bold, brassy, beautiful Susan, who calmly stole extra milk and later, food, and threatened anyone who tried to bother the pair of them. Susan was as beautiful as she herself was in an entirely different way. Only the outgoing Susan could have manipulated, cajoled, and threatened to keep the meanness away from Teddy while Lana helped him survive.

He grew slow and stayed small, while Susan, who was a hell of an actress, somehow intuited that Teddy needed a purpose, an explanation, to survive. Susan was smart that way, so she made up a story to tell him about his purpose on Earth. Somehow, Lana and Susan knew the story was real. Maybe somebody, an angel, sent the story to Susan to tell Teddy.

Lana listened each time Susan explained to Teddy how he was a little spiritual boy in a whole bunch of his past lifetimes, studying spirits' habits and ways on Earth. Then this lifetime showed up, and he thought he was free of learning about the ways of spirit on Earth, which had become boring, so he threw a tantrum when he found out he was alive here again. He was still throwing a temper tantrum and wanting to die this life time, but his soul was thinking about sticking around for the big blowout. Blow up, whatever. And, Lana and Susan were angels in disguise, sent to help him.

She told his story to him when he fussed. When he couldn't stop being sick and crying, Lana turned the tiny television to the only church service she could find and sat him in front of it. It was a Catholic service and he stopped crying immediately, and watched in fascination.

Teddy accepted Susan's story about his spiritual beginnings and began the long process of mending. As he slowly grew well, his fear left him piece by piece, and his breathing improved. Susan told him his soul must have decided to stick around, and that's why he was getting better and would keep on getting better. Maybe he would grow up to be Priest Smith or Rabbi Smith, or Pope Smith, she told him.

The next few years, he grew up, crawling slowly and fearfully and desperately along, clinging to Lana's hand and to Susan's story. Susan embellished the story over time. She told him his soul was slowly mending its tantrum ways and giving up its naughtiness, and starting to like chocolate again. It already liked soft drinks. He laughed, intrigued. The three of them kept his made-up birth story secret from everyone else.

On that day so long ago, she'd left the red cactus desert and driven until she found a cheap motel. She holed up in it until her bruises were mostly gone, bought new clothes, then ditched the '53 Austin Healy. It was a beautiful little car, zesty and light. Strange thing was, she never worried one single minute of the time it took to get her new bearings and start over. Something old and dangerous had stopped stalking her out in that red cactus desert. She'd left it there, and both she and the red cactus knew it.

She left the cheap motel and fled north, leaving the desert and its wisdom behind, knowing the man and girl at the gas station had somehow set her on a new path. They were angels, that's all there was to it.

She drove north, headed for the little house hidden in the woods. She was going home.

"After Christmas, I'll find Susan the big shot author, writer, betrayer. She'll lead me to Teddy. At gunpoint, if necessary," she thought, picturing the little derringer stashed behind the papers in the glove box as she parked the turquoise and white 1951 Ford Victoria in front of the little house hidden deep in the woods. She didn't know that Susan was still taking care of Teddy or that Teddy Smith was living in another country, chanting, carrying a beggar's bowl, and completely happy. She would find Susan as soon as she recuperated.

But it happened the other way around.

Lana was surprised when the phone rang. She never gave her personal house number out to anyone. It was the same number as Miss Charlotte Olivia Masters' private phone, the one she'd listened in on back in the orphanage days. She'd used every means to blackmail Miss Charlotte Olivia Masters into letting her keep Teddy alive, including weird phone calls. That same Miss Charlene Olivia Masters had been dead for years when she'd written the phone number on the back of an old picture of herself she gave to Susan. She'd taken the number as her permanent, private telephone number at her house.

No, it couldn't be.

But it was. Susan found Lana first. All because of the phone number written in schoolgirl pencil on the back of a faded photo stashed in a small, ancient photo album.

Susan saved very few things from her past. She didn't want to remember those years. But she kept a picture of each of the two friends she'd made in the orphanage in the album. It bothered her that she was helping Serena, but she didn't know where Lana was. She wanted to help her. To tell her about Teddy.

She kept the small, brown album tucked in the back of her closet in a shoebox. One day she sat down and opened it again. It was years since she'd looked through its skimpy contents. The album cracked and creaked open. Browned pages stuck together. She carefully pulled them apart. Inside was a photograph of Miss Charlotte Olivia Masters' Home for Orphans, one of Serena, and one of Lana. That was it.

She pulled the photos of Serena and Lana loose, planning to dump the old album and put their pictures in the new one she'd bought. She tossed the old album and the picture of the orphanage in the fireplace and watched it burn. She was glad she'd never see it again. After the album turned to ashes, she examined the pictures of Serena and Lana. On the back of Lana's picture was a phone number. She recognized it. It was Miss Charlotte Olivia Masters' private number. The one she'd memorized and called, disguising her voice. She'd called over the years until someone else answered and told her Miss Charlotte Olivia Masters had passed on.

She dialed the number, thinking of it as a joke, hoping Miss Charlotte Olivia Masters would answer the phone from the bowels of hell and tell her how she liked it there. But when she dialed the number, lo and behold, Lana Ellis answered. It turned out that Lana owned a small house tucked in a little backwoods northern Podunk town where it snowed most of the year. Everyone in that little Podunk Town knew her as the widow Mrs. Smith who'd married a soldier boy who got himself killed off in the war.

Lana held on to the little place through thick and thin. She'd hired a local woman to clean the house every three months and keep the utilities and phone bill paid when she wasn't there. She told the woman she was traveling with her family. Later, when she knew she wasn't going to leave again, she killed her family off in her reminisces with the townspeople.

Susan listened and read between the lines while Lana caught her up on the years. Lana bought the house sight unseen with money she'd earned, and she'd lucked out. It turned out to be a nice, small place. She'd waitressed, then moved to dancing in clubs. She'd saved every penny and bought the little house hidden away in Podunk Town so she could make a home for her and Teddy someday.

But the years passed as she moved up the ladder into becoming a call girl, then dropping that for taking on a boyfriend here and there. But her picker was off and stayed off. She consistently chose the wrong boyfriends so she quit them all. It was time to move to her paid for—but never seen before—secret home and live off the cash she'd stashed in the tiny local bank. Someday she'd go find Teddy.

She moved in and got a job in a small town a few miles away as a waitress. The other waitresses were as close as she came to having friends. She kept her home and private life away from them, but lately, the loneliness of her life was making her sick. She kept catching colds. The doctor checked her over.

"You need to get out more. Go have some fun."

"What?" she was offended.

"I'm not going to treat you for depression," he stated firmly. "Find whatever is bothering you, settle it out, and get on with your life."

She couldn't. She didn't know why. She paced the floor of her tiny house, fighting off the emptiness surrounding her. She couldn't go back. She couldn't go forward either. Not even for Teddy. She was stuck. She worked and saved money, hoping a day would come that she would get unstuck again. She worked and waited. And one day, long after she'd settled into her dull routine, the phone rang, and it was Susan.

She told Susan everything, then she remembered Teddy. She jerked the derringer out of the drawer in the table beneath the phone and fired off a shot.

"Watch out, you'll lose a toe!" Susan shouted at her, laughing.

"You always were gun-crazy! Put that thing away!"

"Where's Teddy?" Lana shouted into the phone.

"Wherever you are, I'm coming to take him away from you and bring him back to the house I bought for us! I will find you!"

Susan laughed. A deep, happy, rolling belly laugh. Lana listened. Yep. That was Susan, all right.

"Well, Dearie," Susan purred in her famous voice, always hoarse from smoking, which she'd given up, but wouldn't admit, "Ah'm still right here. Here's ma' address."

"I don't want your goddamn address. I want to know where Teddy is. Is he with you?" she shouted breathlessly into the phone in a pain filled, accusing voice.

Calmly Susan said, "He's in Tibet. Carrying a beggar's bowl and very happy. At least for the time being."

She listened to Lana exhale.

"I had to get him out of there. When Miss Charlotte Olivia Masters found out who his parents really were, she was determined to tie him up legally in every way as much as possible. Hell, she wanted to adopt him. Then she planned to kill him off. You know how his health has always been poor, at the least, iffy.

So I kidnapped him. My staff and I nursed him back to health, and the only thing he wanted after he found out who he was and that his family was looking for him was to flee. He didn't want that life. As rich as they are, they would have found him if he'd stayed in this country. We both agreed that they would kill him off, given his frail health, and take his huge inheritance. He needed a spiritual place to hide out, to stay strong. So, I got busy and consulted with a few people and voila! a monk in Tibet named Choden will not be noticed."

She waited while Lana took the information in.

"So, Teddy is safe?"

"Yes."

"Why don't you come over here, and we'll talk everything out?" Susan drawled in a smooth, syrupy voice. Lana snorted.

"You make it sound like it's just down the street."

"I can send James, my driving assistant, for you. He's been on plenty of cross country road trips."

"You mean you have a chauffeur?"

"Full-time," Susan answered smugly. "And, he lives in one of my guesthouses. So does Serena."

"Serena from the... old place?" She refused to say orphanage.

"Yep. Why don't you come and join us? Stay as long as you want. Forever if need be."

Her nonchalant statement told Lana everything. Mainly, that Susan still loved her. She inhaled as she slowly realized that Susan probably loved forever.

"I'm sort of worn out. Got the flu or something. Had it awhile."

Tears filled her eyes.

"I have to recuperate. Can't make decisions. Not for years. Been waitressing. I have to see a doctor."

"Don't do anything yet. I'll call you right back."

Susan hung up. Lana stared at the phone then laid it back in its cradle. She drifted to the couch and lay down. Teddy was safe! After a while, the phone rang again. Groggily, she struggled to her feet, crossed to the phone, and answered it.

"James will be there day after tomorrow, early in the morning. About four. I've lined up a doctor and a nurse if you need them. Mrs. Clouse, my housekeeper, is coming with James. She's an older lady. She'll take care of you while James drives you back here. Pack everything. I just need your address."

Lana pulled the receiver away from her ear and stared at it.

She put it back to her ear. "Mrs. Claus? Like in Santa's wife?"

Actually, her name is spelled C-l-o-u-s-e, but yeah, she looks just like Santa's wife, and nice."

"Santa Claus's wife is coming to get me? Well."

Lana repeated her address into the phone, hung up, wandered back to the couch, lay down, and fell asleep.

She slept most of the next two days. She answered the soft knock on the door and wandered back to the couch. Mrs. Clouse finished her packing, and James closed up the house and left notes for the cleaners and the caretaker.

Mrs. Clouse held her a large part of the way to Susan's. James was soft-spoken, kind, deliberate, and distant. They stopped for the night somewhere, she didn't remember where. Just that the long black car was warm inside, and it was cold outside. That soft white sheets covered a large bed so vast that

Mrs. Clouse slept in it with her. At one point, she found herself sobbing in Mrs. Clouse's soft, chubby arms. Her cries were weak at best. Mrs. Clouse spoke soothing words.

If James heard them, he never let on. James slept in the living room of their rentals on a cot the hotel provided. He never mentioned her appearance or her emotional ups and downs. He stayed stalwart, reliable, and comforting, ignoring her weak ravings at odd moments about how evil all men were.

She remembered the sound of gravel on a long driveway before the car stopped. She heard the sound of Susan's big husky laugh as she yanked the car door open and looked inside at Lana.

Consternation, replaced by concern, fled across Susan's face. Lana saw it but said nothing. What could she say? She grinned weakly at Susan. Hands helped her out of the car and through a portal of some kind. Inside, all was blinding white and red. She felt herself being led somewhere, to a quiet, dark place with another huge bed. She fell into it and heard herself fall down into a deep sleep. She knew because she heard herself snore. She laughed silently somewhere inside. Yep. She would never make a prissy, perfect fairy tale beauty. But then, Susan wouldn't either. She giggled weakly. She was too earthy and too sensual. Her body kept her from it with farts and snores and sometimes, beat ups. She slipped into the peaceful, waiting darkness.

Lana was healing. It was slow because the healing needed to take place on many levels of her mind, soul, and emotions, not just in her physical body. They were all connected to each other. Doctors, a massage therapist, a talk therapist, and a nutritionist came and went, along with others. Mrs. Clouse helped her bathe and get ready for each day. She wouldn't let anyone else see her without clothes.

The days flew by as Lana improved. She began meeting Susan in the kitchen to drink fruit teas in the early mornings. They sipped and talked around each other's ways and ideas without coming out with much. They'd been apart awhile. It would take time to catch up. Lana suspected that Susan, who always dove right into the heart of the matter with her friends, had been advised to keep to the edges. They talked about the weather and different kinds of food and other safe things.

As time went on, they spent more time together, watching television, listening to the radio. After a while, they began walking the grounds together with James and the bodyguards discreetly hovering out of hearing range.

At last Lana told Susan about her old life and how the red cactus desert changed her life path. She told Susan about the sacred, holy energies that came and saved her life at the red cactus desert, and how they set her on a different path. She told Susan about shooting holes in the red cactus and how the energies changed into holy, sacred, badass, excellent, mighty warrior energies. How even though she'd gotten in trouble again, she'd been helped out by a man and a young girl out in the desert at a little white church that was renovated into a gas station. She was never the same again.

She told Susan because she was filled with gratitude for them and for this wonderful woman who was her friend. She started crying and tried to fall to her knees, but Susan jerked her back up and roughly scrubbed the top of her head. They used to call it a head burn back in the orphanage, a thing Lana despised. She stopped crying and shouted.

"Why did you do that?"

Susan grinned and moseyed on. Lana followed. After a few minutes of silent walking, Susan said, "Maybe we should go there for Christmas."'

"Where?"

Susan laughed. They kept walking. Susan shoved her hands into her coat pockets.

"To the red cactus desert, of course, silly. Hmmmm...There are sacred chakras all over this planet. Maybe that place is some sort of holy chakra place no one knows about. So, I'm curious. I wrote about a sacred gathering chakra- spot in "Journey to Christmas," remember? It was a sort of like a "making it to the manger" story."

Lana didn't answer. Susan glanced at her. Evidently, Lana hadn't read in a while. "Maybe we should go for Christmas. You've been here almost a year, you know. Christmas will be here before we know it."

Susan laughed as Lana's mouth opened and closed. She wheedled.

"Maybe we could decorate them? Give them thanks for what they did for you?"

Lana snorted. Susan sounded like a priest trying to force a confession out of a sinner. She sounded like that salesman she'd watched giving a fast pitch to a drunken cowboy at a rodeo.

Lana said softly, "I can't go back there. To the little desert store. Never again. I'm sure they'd remember me, and all hell would break loose. They might even call the cops on me."

"Well, that was a long time ago. Besides, we don't have to stop at the store. We can celebrate Teddy's good health there, too, since it's a holy place," Susan answered.

"Well, I thought of it first."

Susan grinned at her.

Lana amended, "I mean, there's been a few times I've thought of going back there."

"Well, let's do it!" Susan exclaimed and laughed.

They linked arms and laughed together. Lana was thinking. Well, this Christmas, it looked like she might find that red cactus desert again and decorate the cactus in gratitude for the new lease on life they'd given her. They deserved it. She'd stay the hell away from the little desert store where she'd almost shot the man. She knew without a doubt they'd remember her and maybe call the cops. She chuckled as she remembered leaving the gas cap behind and not paying for the gas. She liked that she could laugh again. Life had been a hell of a comedy of errors and miracles ever since for her! The cactus, the girl and the man had saved her life. Now Susan Sugar Diamond was helping save the inner parts of her.

÷

The two-lane blacktopped highway was deserted. Susan Sugar Diamond and Lana Ellis grinned at each other as Susan gave the T-Bird the gas. The speedometer soared. They threw their heads back and laughed as they sped through the cold desert air and past the desert store. Lana glanced over at Susan. Susan was concentrating on driving. They were on their way through the New Mexico desert in Susan's classic robin's egg blue '57 Ford Thunderbird. Lana shivered and smoothed her hand over the smooth white leather of the elegant, powerful little blue T-Bird. They were both classic car enthusiasts and loved speed. Yes, she'd caught Susan up to speed on everything. Almost.

They were getting close. Lana said, "Slow down, Susan! I need to watch for the turn-off."

Susan slowed the T-Bird down to a crawl. They found the turn-off with no trouble. Lana's memory of the exact location was perfect. A few minutes later, Susan slid the T-Bird to a stop in the sand. It was cold. The air was vibrating like it was waiting for something. They sat still for a couple minutes.

Finally, Lana said, "This is it." Her throat was dry. She swallowed a couple times.

Susan waited for her to get her bearings. Susan was wise like that. Lana was grateful. Susan was a mouthy steamroller with adept edges. Flexible and knowing. Mostly.

This was Lana's holy place. The only one. Ever. She grabbed her thermos and sipped. Then she opened the door of the little blue T-Bird and slipped out. She heard Susan get out.

"You want to go first?" Susan asked. Lana shook her head no. Arm in arm, they crossed the curved, sandy ridge to the other side. Weaving back and forth, they stood in front of the red cactus. After a long silence, Susan started laughing.

Six red cactus made of wood standing in a row, all newly painted, propped up in tall tin containers, with angry red faces and fists raised to the sky. The six red cacti bore new coats of fire engine red paint and lots of fresh bullet holes. Lana remembered laughing the same way when she first saw the red cactus. Susan, the blonde kewpie with a heart of gold and a mind Wall Street envied, owned a holster filled with both verbiage and bullets. This place was Lana's Christmas gift to Susan. She watched and waited until Susan realized there was more going on in this place than met the eye.

"Holy Jumper Cables!" she muttered, turning in a circle. "You were right. This IS a sacred place! My kind of badass energies here. Yay!"

Lana whooped. The sound echoed. The last time she was here, she'd been crazed with anger and defeat. She'd shot up the red cactus. That's what they wanted. And needed. Anger and rage and the negative things people did were gourmet food to them. She turned to Susan, who was carrying on about vortexes of energy and such, and grabbed her. She shook her until Susan stopped talking and looked at her.

"You got it backwards. They need your anger, your rage, your bad shit, whatever negatives you got. I'm gonna' leave you here to give 'em some. But hurry up. I'm gonna' go get the gun and ammo out of the glove box."

She crossed the sand ridge, heading back towards the T-Bird. She listened to the silence, then to Susan cursing and yelling, unloading old bad memories of stuff she'd gone through and hated for the benefit of the red cactus.

Lana waited by the car until she heard Susan's voice wind down. Then she grabbed the gun and ammo and headed back over the ridge. The cacti were gleaming. Taking a wide-legged stance, she aimed. Then it was Susan's turn. When the boxes of bullets were gone, they went back to the T-bird and collected the pretty, new Christmas ornaments they'd brought from out of the trunk.

They carried them back over the ridge, decorated the red cactus, and stood back. The red cactus looked festive. The Christmas balls and other decorations wired onto them were bright and cheerful. They shone in the winter sun, reflecting the goodwill of the cactus to all and sundry that might show up. At least for a while, Lana thought. She watched as a wire lengthened and drooped. An ornament fell off. The rest of the red cactus began shedding their lovely ornaments. A sour stench filled the air. Susan held her nose.

"Pee-ugh! Oh hell, that's right! They don't like the positive pretties. They're not goody goodies. They're badass bad goodies. We should have put on whatever negative..."

Susan ran across the ridge and looked around. She returned with matches, an oily rag, a tin can, and a rusty flashlight. She found a rock and dented the flashlight and tin can and lit a match and burned an edge of the oily rag. Then she wired the rusty flashlight, the dented tin can and the oily, dirty rag to three of the cactus. They stood back and watched. The three cacti perked right up.

Lana left and returned with a broken beer bottle neck, a rusty beer bottle opener, a bent tin can lid, and added them to the other three red cacti. They perked right up, too.

Filled with inspiration, they both raced back over the ridge and together, dragged a rusty old front grill of a car across it and up to the red cactus. They laid it down in front of them and backed off. The red cactus glowed with delight.

"Bet ya' didn't think you were getting such a big Christmas gift, did ya'?" Susan shouted to the cactus. "Christmas is my specialty!"

The red cactus glistened. They laughed again and ran to find more gifts for them. Later, they strutted back across the ridge to the T-Bird, filled with sacred, badass warrior energy.

"Okay. We're out of here," Lana said.

"Well, maybe not just yet?" Susan answered in a wheedling voice. "Let's drive past the store again," she wheedled with a wicked grin. "It's been years. Nobody remembers you. Let's just drive by. We won't stop."

Lana nodded reluctantly. They rode slowly by the scene of Lana's almost crime. The store had a motel behind it now and other buildings. And a new sign that read Cowboy Johnson's Desert Oasis. Susan did a U-turn just past it and headed back.

"We're stopping at the store," she announced.

Lana shouted, "No!" and grabbed for the steering wheel.

*

Timmon stood on the front porch staring down the empty blacktopped highway. It was three days before Christmas. It was freezing. He'd never seen it this cold. He hugged himself in the flat, blowing wind, pulling his coat closer. Perry had just called. He was delayed. He wouldn't get here today. He didn't know when he'd be in, exactly. There was something he wasn't telling Timmon, and they both knew it. But Timmon didn't press him. He left it alone. He had a feeling he'd have his hands full soon enough.

The freezing, sharp wind stayed low and flat to the ground, stirring up the desert dust. He heard the store door shut behind him. Hector and Annie came out on the porch and stood beside him. They all stared down the empty highway, wondering what to do next until the robin's egg blue '57 Thunderbird came into view.

The three of them watched, open-mouthed as the beautiful eggshell blue Thunderbird slowly wove back and forth across the highway, crept past the gas pumps, turned, and ran straight into the garage wall.

Timmon heard a loud crack as the hood popped open. The engine shuddered to a stop. Bemused, he watched as the two women in the car shouted at each other. He was reminded of a blue robin's egg cracking open and a little bird popping out, yelling for food. Only it wasn't spring. And this robin's egg held two shouting older females.

He ran down the steps, followed by Hector and Annie. They helped the two ladies out of the car. They both looked to be in their late fifties or early sixties. One was small and curvy, with white-blonde hair, the other was a tall, wide-hipped, straight-haired brunette. Apparently, neither one of the ladies was hurt. They ignored their helpers and kept laughing and shouting at each other.

"You liar!" one roared at the other. The other one laughed back at her.

"Yeah! You need your head examined!"

“I couldn’t help myself! I had to do it!”

Timmon and Hector led them up the front porch steps and into the store while they gabbled at each other.

“Don’t worry! I won’t tell your secret, even though it started right here!”

Timmon hesitated. What the hell were they talking about? He was certain he’d never seen either one of them before. He gently seated them at the long counter, stepped behind it, and poured them each a cup of fragrant, hot coffee.

“What do you mean, ladies?” he interrupted, sliding the thick white cups of coffee under their noses, and waited. Because of his keen sense of smell, he’d experimented until he changed the ordinary, mundane mud that was once served at the desert store into an exotic, fabulous blend of thin, fragrant pleasure. He kept the blend his secret and took out a patent on it. He called it The Desert Store Brew. As of yet, he didn’t have any desire to sell it in any way. It belonged here, to the desert store, to the store’s misfits and to their dreams. Both women stopped talking. Astonished looks flew over their faces. They bent to their coffee cups, sniffing like hungry dogs on a scent.

“Wow! Heavenly!” the one resembling a kewpie doll with a hoarse voice exclaimed. They lifted their cups to their lips and sipped. The kewpie doll’s eyes widened. She put her cup down and groaned to the Amazon sitting beside her, “Oh my God! Delicious!”

The Amazon merely nodded and sipped again.

"Got anything to go with it?" she asked in a husky voice as her eyes roamed over the store.

"Sandwiches." Timmon grinned in relief. "Annie, take over, will ya?"

"You ladies sure you're okay? Don't need a doctor or anything?"

They looked at each other guiltily and shook their heads no.

"Well, then me and Hector are going to see about getting your car into the garage. It will take a few days to get it fixed, I'm thinking."

He waited.

"I guess we're stuck here. I'm Susan Sugar Diamond, and this is my sidekick, Lana Ellis," the kewpie doll said with no remorse, only glee.

Timmon nodded.

"Annie, please assign the ladies motel rooms three and four. Unless you want to bunk in together?"

He waited until they shook their heads no.

"I don't think the T-Bird will be ready before Christmas. We have to get someone out here to look it over, then we'll know more. They may have to take it into Albuquerque to fix it. Any objections, ladies?"

They shook their heads in unison.

"None."

He didn't ask them why they ran into the garage wall. At this point, it wouldn't do any good. Maybe later.

I bet ya's I can sen'
a' body' down ta' Hell
All it takes is da' truf'
or the biggest damn lie
ya' evah tol' ta' inybody.

Part Four

Perry helped Avery stay hidden because he knew Dawn's daughters drowned their brother, but their father insisted on believing their lies. Perry helped Avery hide by hiring lookouts to prevent snoops. Their bull-headed, opinionated father wouldn't listen to one word against Dawn or her daughters. And he never would have, not until he accidentally caught them laughing at him for believing their lies about Carlton's death. Talk about having to be hit over the head. Ironically, their filthy secret came out shortly after Avery died...

Matthew Mark Judson

Matthew Mark Judson confessed everything to his son Perry. About staying hidden and eavesdropping until Dawn and her daughters Denise and Debbie thoroughly exhausted the subject of Carlton's death and the lovely meal ticket he was providing them with because of it. They planned to keep him paying the rest of his life.

They never knew he'd changed his mind about the trip he was supposed to leave on, that instead, he'd gone in search of them to try once again to get some relief, any relief, from the guilt and pain over Avery drowning their beloved son and brother, Carlton. They carried pictures of Carlton with them and pulled them out frequently to mourn him when he was around. He knew they relied on him to comfort them, but he wasn't good at it. So, he gave them things. Clothes. Convertibles. Cash. Whatever they wanted. Their devastation over Carlton's death never let up, leaving him constantly at their mercy, causing him to cave to every whim they came up with.

They placed portraits of Carlton in every room of the mansion he owned where Avery drowned him. Then they traveled. They said it was to get away from the unhappy memories, so he gave in. This latest place was on the French Riviera.

What an unhappy life I've been forced to lead—all because of Avery! Matthew thought resentfully. He sighed. He was too early for his business flight. He decided not to leave until he spoke with Dawn. There was plenty of time. He snorted to himself. *I mean, grovel to her again.* He set his suitcases down and strode through the villa in search of her, a hangdog expression on his face. He'd do whatever they wanted him to do, once again. And the next time, too. *Oh, Avery, why did you do it?* he thought for the millionth time.

He sighed and slowed his steps. He followed the sound of Dawn and her daughters' voices until he was almost in the huge drawing room they lounged in. He paused in surprise at their sudden laughter. They never laughed around him. Hope rose in him. Maybe things were changing for the better at last! Puzzled, he stopped and listened.

Then he heard Carlton's name and froze. Not again! Then Avery's name. His head drooped sorrowfully. Then his name and more laughter? What? Curious, he instinctively stepped behind a floor-length, full-curtain swaying in the Mediterranean breeze in the villa Dawn, Denise and Debbie insisted he take for a few months until they tired of it. He stood behind the swaying curtain on the edge of the drawing room, still as a statue of marble, listened, and at last, learned.

Tears flowed down his face while shock and rage whitened it. Yes, he'd hid and listened and learned. When they were finished damning him and his, they swept past the curtain he stood behind, never suspecting that he was behind it. When they were gone, he stepped out from behind the curtain a changed man.

Their words had at last set him free from their vile prison. Unsuspecting, they'd handed his life back to him. Their secret, spiteful words had set his soul free of the guilt stalking him every day of his life. He snatched his packed suitcases out of the hallway and sneaked them into his office, locking the door behind him, something he never did, for he always gave them full access to him, night and day, out of guilt. They'd flung the door open many times when he was working just to interrupt him and upset him with rants about poor Carlton, and he'd let them. No more. It was over. His heart sang, beating fast with both jubilation and rage. His son was not a murderer! Never was! They were! The lying bitches! He wanted to murder them!

He poured himself a stiff drink and paced the floor until the permanent pity party he'd kept going for himself for years began dissipating. His mind began clearing, sorting it out, working properly again for the first time in years, moving past the lies, past his misery, connecting the dots. Hours later, he understood everything clearly. His mind made up, with mixed anger and relief, he moved on. He began sorting out the new man he would be now, picking up pieces, dropping others, putting them together in a resurrection of his life, learning what it was he should do.

He was a man who prided himself on his craftiness, so he changed his plans, small pieces at a time. He'd suspected for a long time that they listened in on his phone calls. He remembered things they knew that they couldn't have known without listening in on his calls. Things that now no longer seemed as coincidental as they insisted.

Near dusk that same day, without ever seeing them again, he picked up his luggage, slipped out of the office and the villa, and carried it to his Mercedes. The place was quiet. The women were either in a different part of the huge villa or out somewhere. They liked to party and be written up in the society pages—things he avoided.

He placed his luggage in the trunk and drove away. At the French airport, he booked a flight for America and called Perry.

"Come home to 1227 California. We need to talk. In person."

He left the three bitches at the villa and never looked back. He flew back to the mansion where they'd drowned Carlton. Dawn, Denise and Debbie had guilted him into holding on to the property when he wanted to sell it, when he needed more than anything to just forget and move on. But they'd whined about the memories of the son and brother they'd lost because of his son Avery, the murderer. They'd gripped him by the balls for years—until now. Until he'd accidentally eavesdropped. He paced the floor of his house, waiting for Perry's return.

Perry didn't tell his father about Avery. Not yet. He couldn't. Not until the large wreck of a man pacing back and forth in front of him was alive again with his six-foot-something frame and great mane of hair standing back up again. Not until his white mane of hair was glossy again, and he began changing his shirts several times a day instead of never. Not until his roars could be heard as far as the south pole once more. Perry winced. Maybe they could do without that one being restored.

There'd been no more slaps or temper tantrums after Carlton drowned. Just the wreck of the Hesper, his father, kissing the nasty three women's asses and whining about everything, letting his businesses go all to hell. *Good thing he'd been there to step in and take the reins,* thought Perry. Dawn, Denise and Debbie avoided him as much as possible. They were cool and secretive when forced to spend any time with him. They knew he suspected their big secret, so they surrounded Matthew whenever he was around. No private time between father and this son allowed. He'd given up and taken over the businesses, which kept him from thinking about it much. They all left him alone and on his own because he brought in the money.

÷

William called Perry shortly after Avery died.

"What is it, William?" Perry asked. "I'm in the middle of something."

"Well, Perry. Avery's gone," William drawled in a trembling old voice. Perry's heart sank.

"Gone where?" he asked the question, though he already knew the answer. He just didn't want to hear it yet.

"He died, Perry. Just yesterday. In the middle of the day. At the desert store. Of a heart attack."

"What? No! I don't believe it!" Perry shouted in pain and grief. William stayed on the phone with him long enough to ask him to not tell Matthew yet. Perry agreed. Neither one of them said what they were thinking. That it would break their hearts to have

Matthew Mark Judson say he didn't give a damn about his son Avery, whom they both always loved so fiercely.

"I don't want him coming out to the desert store and raising hell with Mama, Avery's woman. She can't deal with his kind of personality at all. She's too fragile right now." Perry understood.

÷

Perry and Matthew laid out a plan to get revenge. Perry was only too happy to consult with their lawyers on behalf of his father right under the noses of the three spiteful women who always kept a hawk-eye on Matthew. Normally, Perry avoided Matthew like the plague, but this situation called for close contact. His father was a changed man, but not a better one, Perry soon realized. The angry, obsessed man was replaced by a man full of pity for himself, a man filled with endless rage that blamed everyone else. Perry didn't like the before or the after version of Matthew Mark Judson.

Perry asked Matthew to act even more hangdog and sorry around Dawn and her daughters, hoping they might get careless and gloat behind his back even more. Matthew and Dawn hadn't slept together in years; that made it easier for him to hide his dislike and contempt for her. Besides, she was always having a fling with one or another of the hired help. He'd become impotent for awhile after Carlton drowned and couldn't make love to Dawn anyway.

She'd used that as an excuse to start sleeping around. He looked the other way while she played around, believing she was having affairs because she needed him, and he couldn't do it.

He'd address that problem later.

A bit at a time, Perry discreetly brought in professionals to wire certain rooms in their houses with the best equipment money could buy to record and monitor the three bitches. Matthew lowered himself into the dregs to get the job done, knowing each time that they would go away and laugh at him. And that once in a while, they would gather together somewhere and secretly gloat over and whisper about the hold they had on him. It took time to get it all done, to record their rare and gloating conversations confessing to Carlton's drowning.

At last, they had what they needed. Matthew hired the best of the best to draw up an airtight legal case. He planned to present it to them in a special way.

His team of people went to work, sealing the three women up in ironclad legalities that prevented them from ever making a peep about him or his family. He would see to it that their emotional blackmail of him cost them plenty. It was the finest document he'd ever planned.

Matthew Mark Judson waited until the three bitches were sitting at a table out on the back lawn of his house in the Hamptons, sharing mid-afternoon tea. He gave the signal, and the waiting lawyers moved in. The women's smug faces turned in surprise toward the two handsome young lawyers approaching them.

He watched their sexual greed rise as they offered the two handsome young lawyers food, drinks, and to be seated. The lawyers remained standing. He watched from behind a curtain, as he did in the beginning when he first discovered what they were. He watched the smug, greedy looks slide from the three women's faces as they read the papers the aloof young lawyers handed them.

He'd caught them by surprise. The legal papers offered proof of their guilt and a divorce settlement in which he would settle a small yearly amount on Dawn and her daughters. He offered Dawn a small house in France, paid for, in a small French village. Otherwise, he would take them to court and smear their names all over the tabloids for murder. None of them were to marry, or the scandal would surface. No other man deserved to go through the hell he'd suffered because of their greed and cruelty.

Denise and Debbie, if they chose to live with their mother, would receive small yearly allowances. He wanted them to stay together, stewing in their own brew of lies and hates, helpless before him, hurting each other instead of other people with their never-ending slyness and cruelties. He knew they could not and would not stop being the way they were. They were murderers. And sooner or later, they would surface again, and he would have to deal with their evil once more. He'd stay prepared.

They packed and left swiftly, finally afraid. They knew they'd pushed him too far. He listened to the recorded plans they made behind his back. They would give in for now, move to the house in France, and reconnoiter. Whatever. Evil always rose again in some form. He would deal with it then, now that he knew what they were.

They left in a hurry. When the house was empty, Perry called in cleaning crews. Quickly their rooms were stripped and fumigated. All of their pictures and personal effects were thrown out. The house stood empty and clean. It was over. Perry suggested Matthew put the house of misery up for sale as soon as possible. He would handle the sale.

He suggested that Matthew move to their beach house for a while. Matthew agreed. He was grateful and relieved. But his rage hung on, causing him to sink into a giant pity-party of his own making. He walked endless miles of sand, hoping the roar of the ocean would displace his rage. It didn't. He thought constantly of Avery. He remembered, and he suffered. He never treated Avery very well. He'd neglected him, even before the "accident" took place. He wondered what Avery's life was like, and where he was now.

He hurt and raged and stayed angry until he sickened. He quit eating, and his weight fell away from him. The whole ordeal was taking a great toll on him. He was a changed man. His hatred seethed on, slimming him down, weakening him further. Finally, he realized he was going to need help overcoming it if he wanted to live. When he was well enough again, he would see to Avery. Meanwhile, Perry was still handling all their business dealings. He'd taken them over years ago and was busy or gone most of the time.

Matthew called Perry.

"Perry, I am dying of my own hate. Once it got unleashed, it went wild. It won't stop, no matter what I do. I can't get free of my shackles. I'm nearly down to skin and bones."

He waited in silence following his announcement. Then he asked, "Is there anything you know of that I can do to stop it?"

Perry still didn't answer.

Matthew said softly, "I apologize to you for the cruelties I inflicted upon you and Avery when you were growing up. I will do anything to make it up to both of you."

He gusted out a huge sigh.

"Damn! I hate this frickin' atonement business! It sticks in my craw! What a hell of a life!"

Perry finally said, "I'll call an old friend and get back with you... Father."

Perry never claimed him as "father." Just Matthew. It sounded so good! Sort of like maybe Perry thought he was a worthwhile project.

Perry called William and explained Matthew's situation. William said, "I'll think about it and call you back."

Perry said, "Father has changed, William. I hope it sticks. I don't know. But I don't want to lose him."

"Okay, but don't tell him about Avery yet. Mama needs more time," William said, and hung up. In a few days, he called Perry back. Hesitantly he said, "There's a special lady who might could help him. Her name is Lily Jean Bloome. Here's her phone number."

Perry heard the hesitancy in Williams' voice.

William said, "I hope he's careful. She's someone very special to me."

"Thank you, William," Perry said. They hung up at the same time.

William stared at the phone. He felt like he'd done something very wrong. He wanted to keep Lily Jean Bloome all to himself. But Avery's father needed help. He sighed. The ways of this world were too complicated to figure out sometimes. "Damn it!" he swore softly.

Lily Jean Bloome

Matthew Mark Judson was madly in love. Soul searing, blasting love. The hatred of Dawn and her daughters was subsiding, overcome by love. The three bitches meekly complied with his every demand. They'd moved to France and were living together in their small house on the tiny income he provided. He knew that given their insatiable appetites for money and cruelty, they would inevitably surface again. He kept working, setting up every way he could to protect himself and his heirs from them.

One day he was walking on his private beach, no one around, his mind busily informing him of the latest dark possibility he might encounter from them. He stopped and sank down to the sand. Enough! He didn't want them killing him off from a distance!

He'd exhausted the standard medical fare offerings, rejecting everything from pills to drug him out, talk therapies, anger management, massage, all of which he thoroughly and loudly rejected. There was a thorn in his side; why not yell about it? He'd fired doctors left and right. Finally, he decided to go see the woman Perry recommended. He guessed she was some sort of psychologist and some other things he didn't listen to when Perry recommended her.

When he set up the appointment, he discovered that her address was just down the beach. He snorted. So, she lived at an expensive beach address, not just vacationed here. He'd pictured an old woman living n a tiny shack, intoning chants over the ocean and writing books about the emotional content of water and sand and whatever. Out of curiosity, he strolled down the beach past her house but discovered nothing except a discreetly high privacy wall with sand-strewn, stubborn ivies winding their tough way up and over the wall.

He went to see Lily Jean Bloome and instantly fell madly and intensely in love. She rejected his hot, intense energies, melting them with steadfast inner calm and cool, clever wisdom, sometimes icy wisdom.

He was a piece of work, and he knew it. Step by step, she gradually steered him around to discovering and owning who he was, who he'd always been. She called him a red Earth warrior, one cast from iron, one from the days of old, one who'd been thrown into whining, puling atonement, into trying to redeem his reckless, meanly lived past lives.

She said the new place he was stuck in was not a natural habitat for a red Earth warrior. In fact, it was a place a red Earth warrior would fight to the death to get out of or run away from. At the least, he would bump into everything, breaking all kinds of stuff—meaning people—in the process. A loud, short sighted warlord with warts. Ugly. With a big appetite. And a heart of gold he didn't want. A warlord with a hidden need to feed and nurture and scold a village of his own, one he didn't want. A warlock with mysteries inside himself still to be revealed. He'd already been given a couple of revelations lately—he needed them—she'd laughed at him!

She gave him new paradigms and roles to pour himself into. But he wanted her, desired her, wanted to bed her. She diverted the river of the insistent, lower chakra, rude energies he sent her into cooling creeks flowing around rocks.

He stayed in love and lust and hid it from everybody but her. But inexorably, changes in him happened. He felt them and didn't like it. He talked about finding himself again. He became filled with simple happiness in odd moments. Moments he couldn't celebrate with booze or pity for himself or shouting. They simply were. He gradually calmed down and came back into himself.

"Hello, you. I see you're back," she said one day to him. He began to accept the odd changes. He breathed better as old shadows were laid to rest.

Lily Jean Bloom never offered him tea or even water. He once asked for water, and she said, "Go home and get some...or do without."

She never gave him anything or let him touch her in any way. No handshakes. Nothing. She gave him no history of herself, no words he could manipulate her with. She knew how crafty his nature naturally was when he wanted something.

He paced and argued out loud about himself, yelling and shouting to himself and her about who he was, what he wanted and how pitifully needy he was, never swaying her while she stood cool and strong, away from him. Her white hair and demeanor were that of a mentor to him, but he lusted for her as a lover. He'd never accepted a mentor, male or female, before. He didn't know how. He knew nothing about the many kinds of absolute love connections waiting in this world to experience.

Tough. She told him. She told him no countless times. She told him he was a tough learner, a rebellious brat who needed to learn how to open his heart chakra, one who insisted on staying in his lower chakras and doing it the hard way. He sneered at her and called her a new ager.

"As if that matters," she'd countered.

He fought for and won the needed changes in himself by himself, and kept winning, so she began distancing the times he could visit. She told him he was a handful, busy fighting against himself and winning and she needed time to recover her energies between his visits. There was absolutely no touching or comfort offered of any kind, even when he whined. He realized he must learn even more or lose her. That was all there was to it.

"You need other teachers, too," she insisted.

He began. Awkward and stumbling, he sought out teachers to tell him why his life, and why life, in general, was so screwed up. No therapists. Just wise people. But not her. He didn't tell her he was busy seven days a week now trying to understand life and himself and to let other people into his world in new ways. It was difficult because his trust was still shattered from Dawn and her daughters. Lily Jean Bloom laughed at him when he told her that.

"That's a bunch of bull crap!" she said. "Get over yourself or die. It's that simple."

Lily Jean Bloom was to be his love someday when he understood himself better. He looked forward to winning the prize. And Avery. He would get him back, too. There was a lot to do. Just as soon as he got his life right side up again. He began to eat better and picked up a little weight.

÷

William never liked Matthew Mark Judson. Not for one minute. He remembered Matthew's steam roller tactics and grew nervous about having referred him to Lily Jean Bloome. He asked her about him, but she just shrugged.

"None of your bees-wax."

He stared at her. She grinned back at him, Light and purity standing in her calm, steady eyes. He knew in that instant that she would never stoop to conquer. In fact, she didn't need to conquer. He didn't hide the love and admiration showing on his face. New hope filled him. A hope for a good life, with or without her being the way he wanted her to be. Pictures. They were misleading. Mostly. You got the essence but mostly didn't understand.

Staring at her, he realized this woman would forever be a part of his life. She held a permanent place in his soul and knew it. Suddenly, he grasped for an instant, just how many ways this woman loved. He became overwhelmed and gasped, reaching out to her. Suddenly, she was in his arms. He was home. She was everything he'd ever dreamed of.

He held her close, making soft, gasping "ah" sounds, running his hands all over her. Hugging her close, tracing all she was with his hands. Like a child finding a lost, beloved Teddy bear. Not letting her go. Innocent embracing of a lost, missing part of himself. Like a child who had found the dearest friend they thought they'd lost forever.

At last he laid his head on her shoulder. He hoped he could stop there, but he couldn't. He sought out the sweet hollow in her neck, and she let him. He kissed it and moaned. She held him gently as he lifted his head to see if what he was doing was okay. She looked into his eyes and stepped back.

"You need to rest."

She took his hand and led him to the bedroom. She lay down on the bed, fully clothed.

"Come here and snuggle up to me. Hold me and rest. Don't go any further than that, or you will interrupt this healing process."

A few minutes later, the sweet peace he'd sought forever overcame him. He felt its sweetness seep through his body and closed his eyes. His bones relaxed. He was home at last. The restless yearning was finally satisfied. He had no clue what was going on, but Lily Jean Bloome knew, and that was enough for him. He trusted this woman in this new way, exploring the freedom it gave him to dream again, forcing the chains of his arthritis loose. He slept for two hours. She never left him, though some part of him knew she was awake.

"Will you go to the desert store with me for Christmas? We can stay out at the ranch," he asked when he woke up. "I ask because there are a couple of special women I'd like you to meet."

"Maybe," she said.

He studied her. She studied him back. "You know what you're doing?" he asked.

"Yes," she said. "Do you?"

"When it comes to you, yes."

She gifted him with a lovely smile.

"Sometimes, I think about moving back to the ranch. Away from California, you know? Maybe you'd be interested?"

"Maybe," she answered. "But I would never give up my home here."

"Well, mebbe' we could go back and forth."

Flushed and pleased with where this was going, he said, "Flapjacks. Can we have some flapjacks? All of a sudden, I'm very hungry. I'll make them."

"Sure." she answered.

Matthew Mark Judson

Matthew called Perry from the big house.

"Come over and have breakfast with me at the big house. Not the beach house," he wheedled. He knew Perry would always have reservations about him, but he was a changed man, if only Perry knew it.

"What are you doing there?" Perry asked sharply. "I thought you were staying at the beach house."

"I have a right to be here. This is my home...one of them," he amended. After a long silence, he heard Perry sigh and grinned silently to himself. He'd won again. He liked to win. Nothing wrong with that.

Perry broke a muffin in half and buttered it sparingly. He looked at the muffins and eggs sitting on the kitchen table and remembered being banished to the kitchen while his father and Dawn dined in grandeur at the long table in the formal dining room. Why did Matthew want to eat in here? What was he up to now? Frankly, he was tired of Matthew's never-ending pity-party, his loud, brash ways that never changed, and mainly the knowledge that Matthew didn't have the ability to see anyone else except in the advantages they held for his personal gain. He sighed and took a small bite of the muffin, reserve showing on his face.

"I want you to spend Christmas with me here. This house will be sold soon and we won't ever be in it again," Matthew said nostalgically, expecting Perry to jump at the chance.

Perry shuddered involuntarily, remembering Christmas's past. Christmas's loaded with loud voices, fake laughter, and orders to be obeyed or else, in this house. He never spent Christmas with Matthew. Not since he was fifteen.

"Sorry. Matthew. I've already made other plans. And I think you should stay out of here. Go back to the beach house. This one already has a good offer on it, considering its reputation," Perry reminded his father, alluding to the biggest problem there was with the sale of this house. Matthew stared at his son, his eyes hardening. This wasn't going the way he planned. No, not at all.

"Why not spend Christmas here with me? What will you be doing?"

"Business. Somewhere else. Maybe in Hong Kong. A meeting. I'll spare you the details."

"Well, I want to hear them," Matthew answered, fuming.

Perry met his glare with his own glare.

"Just stuff."

"You mean you don't want to be with me," Matthew stated.

"That is correct," Perry answered calmly.

"You need to finish up whatever it is you need to do in this..." he waved his arm, "haunted house..." and get the hell out of here while you still can. We're lucky to be able to sell it at all after the bad reputation Dawn, Denise and Debbie worked so hard to grow and maintain. Their yearly pilgrimages back here to this house made it negatively famous, remember? They've made this place almost impossible to sell, which they cleverly planned. As it is, we're going to be lucky to break even."

He stood up from the table, tossed his napkin on it.

"You need to finish up in this house and get the hell out for good."

He turned his back on Matthew and strode away, tossing words back over his shoulder.

"Maybe Lily Jean Bloome can exorcise the demons in this place for you. I can't. And wouldn't if I could."

Perry moved swiftly through the wide double doors to the kitchen and out of sight. Matthew stood up and tossed his napkin on the table and shouted after him, "That's right! Run away again!"

He was hungry. He sat back down and ate. *This isn't over*, he thought. *I wonder what he's up to?"*

He finished eating and drank his coffee. Then he jumped up and strode to his office. Somebody was up to something. It was time to make a few well placed phone calls. These days, he was suspicious of everyone. Who wouldn't be after what Dawn did to him? She'd ruined his life. He had a right to do this, he told himself self righteously...

The phone rang. A male voice answered.

"Jack Bentley here."

Without preamble, Matthew said, "Jack. I need you to find out what Perry is up to these days, and see what he's got planned for Christmas in particular. Right away. As soon as possible."

A weighted silence ran down the line. Matthew waited. Jack was his employee, and he would have his way. Finally, Jack answered him in a voice filled with cold disapproval. "Okay. It's your dollar."

Matthew hung up, disgruntled. Jack sounded disapproving. Maybe it was because their sons were old friends. Perry had spent a few summers palling around with Jack's son's, but that was years ago. Perry always spent any extra time staying away from home, Matthew remembered resentfully. Perry had liked staying at Jack's modest house. Avery did too, until Matthew sent him away, banished him.

It all started because Matthew hired Jack's agency to work for him when both their boys were just kids. He and Jack had volunteered their boys for the same charity project, unbeknownst to each other. The boys met and their friendship took off. So did Avery and Perry. They'd practically moved in at Jack's humble little place with no pool or amenities. He resented it, and he and Jack never progressed beyond their business relationship.

He guessed Jack would never check up on his own sons, that's why he sounded so disapproving. Jack believed his boys had a right to their privacy. But unlike Jack, he was an important man; there were higher standards to maintain. There were the newspapers, his money, and the media forcing him to keep an eye on Perry. And if Jack wouldn't do it, somebody else would, and Jack knew it. Matthew finished his calls and left for the beach house.

Jack called Matthew back a few days later.

"I'd like to drop by to give you the report on Perry."

"You don't have to do that. Just tell me what he's up to."

"Can't do that. Won't."

"Why not?"

"I need to see you in person. It's important."

"All right!" Matthew snarled impatiently.

"Come on over! But make it quick!"

"I'll be right there," Jack said coolly and hung up. The report turned out to be much more than he expected. Jack handed him the file folder and waited for his reaction, a somber look on his face. The report was about both Avery and Perry. Both his sons. His only blood children. Avery was gone. He'd lived out his life in a crummy little desert store in New Mexico. And died there. And Perry was going there for Christmas.

"Get out!" he snarled at Jack as his world fell apart again. Jack stood and left without a word of condolence. Matthew would never allow anyone to see him in such a shape. No sharing. None of their silly assed, fake caring. The pain was huge, too much for him to stand. He paced the floor of the beach house for hours. He drank from the liquor cabinet until he fell into a stupor, then he threw himself down on the large, long leather sofa and passed out.

He mourned his fate, the losses he'd taken, all alone. Perry—that liar—knew Avery was... gone. How long had he known? He couldn't get in touch with him. Perry was in Europe somewhere, busy being incognito to Matthew, a thing he excelled at.

He didn't know how much more he could take. He walked and mourned and stalked up and down the beach and cried and bellowed in his room, then did it all over again, starting at daybreak. He insisted his doctor give him pills for his emotional pain. But he couldn't take them. A sixth sense told him that he would be better off facing his pain than using booze or drugs to numb it.

At last, he remembered Lily Jean Bloome. Both he and his house needed her help desperately. He jerked on a jacket and stumbled out the back door and stumbled down the beach to her home. It seemed to take forever. The sand pulled at his dress shoes and filled them, making his legs feel like lead weights. He thought he'd pulled on flip flops and a tee-shirt, but he guessed he didn't. He rang the doorbell and waited, weaving back and forth, believing he was in so much misery she would no doubt pity him and take him in. But she didn't. When she answered the door, he started shouting, telling her what he was going through. She held up a hand in the age-old signal of stop until she got his attention.

"Go home. Shower. Get dressed. Stay sober. Call me. Make an appointment."

He switched to pleading.

"Can't you see me right now? I'm in the worst shape I've ever been in!" he shouted.

"You heard me."

She shut the door in his face. He listened to the door lock. He stood there, trying to decide whether to pound on the door or go home. He was pissed off. He pounded on the door.

She opened it a crack and said, "Do it again, and I'll call the cops on you. And I'll never accept another appointment with you."

He went home. Stumbling along the beach, running a few steps, then shouting at the sky, waving his fists. Nobody loved him. It was the truth, he thought bitterly. He picked up the phone and called Jack again.

"Tell me more."

"I don't know anymore."

"Well, I need to know more!"

Matthew, ruthless in business, circled his quarry, aiming to take it out on Jack, whether he was innocent or not. Hesitantly, Jack said, "There is another detective who's known the people at Avery's store for years. He's done work for them. He might have that information. His name is Dan Swain. I have his contact number."

Jack hung up on Matthew without his usual curt goodbye after Matthew wrote the phone number down. Matthew glared at the phone. Well, there was nothing further to talk to Jack about anyway. He called the number for Dan Swain. Dan answered.

"Swain Detective Agency. How can I help you?"

Matthew said, "This is Matthew Mark Judson. Perhaps you've heard of me."

He was hoping to intimidate the detective to get what he wanted more easily.

"Maybe have. Maybe not," Swain responded coolly.

Matthew decided to abandon his in intimidation tactics and get right to the point.

"I'm Perry and Avery Mott Judson's father. I know Avery has... is... gone. What I want to find out about is that little desert store and everybody who had anything to do with him. I want them all investigated."

A long silence rolled down the phone line. Matthew waited while Dan Swain digested his request.

"Sorry for your losses, whatever they are, but I don't know those people or anything about any store... or cabin either, for that matter," he added hastily, gabbling on in a smooth, syrupy voice.

His voice changed. In a fake, smooth, high voice, he said, "I have so many environmental cases going on, I can't take on another case of any kind right now. Maybe another time? Keep me in mind, though, if you need future services involving the tracking down of endangered species or people who further illegal mountain climbing. Those people are just plain dangerous."

He hung up on Matthew. Matthew stared at the phone. He didn't believe Swain's story for one minute. He must be in cahoots with the people who hid his son and kept him away from his father. He'd completely forgotten that he was the one who banished his son. Amazing how death could change so many memories. He opened the file again. There was no use calling Jack. He would just be disapproving and evasive. Well, hell. He would just have to go find out for himself. Yes. He would go to Avery's desert store for Christmas.

He called Lily Jean Bloome to book an appointment.

"I will allow you one half-hour. That's it," she responded tersely. They set the day, hour, and time for three days later. By then, he'd sorted through all kinds of stances to take with her in his imagination. He was deeply offended, angry, pitiful, and whiny. He realized woefully that his old charming self had deserted him for the time being. There was nothing to choose from but negative stances. He decided he would just shut up. He showed up on time. She opened the door cautiously.

"Are you planning to behave? If not, if you've got some drama planned, then leave now... and don't come back... and by the way, this is the last time I'm going to see you."

He huffed. Nobody talked to him like this and got away with it! It took a minute, but he gained control of himself admirably. Since he'd already decided that keeping his mouth shut was his best alternative with this woman he adored and lusted after, he didn't say a word. She let him in. Yes, it seemed as if deciding to be mute was a wise choice.

But he couldn't stop himself. He'd spilled his guts, he thought bitterly, walking down the beach back to his house after his session with her. And the time had flown by! He'd told her everything he'd planned not to tell anyone. He'd blabbed about Perry and Avery and how he was going to the desert store for Christmas and sort everyone out. They needed it, he'd told her. Keeping secrets like Avery's... being gone... from him.

"I'll let you know about your house," she'd answered when he asked her to cleanse it of its past.

Lily Jean Bloome

Matthew was gone a few minutes before Lily Jean Bloome could unfreeze. She sighed. Sometimes having the Sight brought on complex situations, but she'd never regretted one minute of the gift she'd been given by Spirit. She made herself a pot of hot fruit tea, poured a cup, and sipped it. She paced the floor, wondering what to do. Finally, she made up her mind. She picked up the phone and called William.

"Well, hell!" he said after she told him what Matthew Mark Judson was planning to do. He sighed. A long silence followed. Lily Jean Bloome knew he was sorting it all out. She waited.

"Guess we just can't stop life from running its course, can we, Lily Jean Bloome?"

"You go on to the desert store. I'll be there just at the right time," she said.

"Thank you, Lily Jean Bloome," William said. "By the way, you could call me William the Dude if you wanted to. The kids do."

Lily Jean Bloome called Matthew.

"About your house... you need to separate from it quickly. And don't go back. Those three women have a hold on your energies through that house, and it's stronger when you are there. It has become their territory, a negative energy vortex—a chakra—they use for their own purposes. They undermine your common sense and escalate your temper when you are in that house. It's easy for them. Stop whining and fighting with forces you know nothing about, let alone how to handle—you're not subtle enough or clever enough to deal with them, so get out. Let me know when you are out for good. Leave me a key to the house and directions to it under my front doormat. If I need anything else, I will contact you. And, I will let you know when it's done."

Well, heah' we go's agin'
down dat' dam lonesome road agin'
ain't seen ya' since doan' kno' when
where ya' been gone ta', honee?

Part Five

Perry

Perry was bone tired from the long drive through the desert. The shocks on the old beat-up station wagon, the only thing available to rent this close to Christmas, were shot, but his ability to stay inscrutable through any situation held him in good stead. He'd withstood many kinds of pain in his life, but nobody would ever know it. He'd make sure of that.

William had called and told him about Avery's woman. About Avery's great love for her. About her simplicity, her Sight, her Goodness, and the roots she'd put down at the desert store. How she was planning to go to California to get some kind of revenge for Avery over Carlton's drowning. She didn't know yet that she wouldn't need to anymore. Dawn was gone. So were her shrewish daughters. William asked him to go to her and stop her before she grieved herself to death. Or murdered someone.

"Go look the place over. It6's different and kind of special. Learn something about your brother, Perry. Give her something of Avery's to hold on to." William urged. “To hell with all this hiding out now. It’s over. Let’s move on and do what is needed.”

So here he was. Perry wondered about his brother’s world and why he chose a damn desert to live in. A place so far away from people. Did he ever heal from his childhood wounds? And what about the ditsy, odd woman he’d left behind, one that stayed so in love with him she could barely live? He made the turn off to the ranch that William described. Cold dust curled up behind the old station wagon as Perry passed the house and came to a stop behind it.

Perry climbed out of the station wagon. William, Lily Jean Bloome, and Emma stepped out the back door of the giant house. William strode toward Perry, a huge grin on his face, his arms extended. They met on middle ground, grabbed each other and embraced.

“Hot damn, Perry! It’s been hell and forever since I last saw you! You look good!” William exclaimed, pulling back and clapping Perry on the back. Perry, who was of a quiet, cautious temperament gained in self-defense in order to fend off his father, answered.

“You look fine too, William.” His eyes searched the women.

“Where’s Avery’s woman? The one they call Mama?”

“She’s gone to a monastery to stay for a while. You’ll meet her later, maybe.”

Lily Jean Bloome and Emma came over and introduced themselves. They all swayed silently in the cold wind, filled with unanswered questions, until Emma said, "I welcome all of you into my home. Let's go inside. It's warm, and there is eggnog and all manner of Christmas delicacies ready to partake of."

Everyone linked arms or held hands, staying close to each other as they headed for the back door.

William thought, "*So, this is one of your surprise Christmas presents, huh Avery? I wonder what else you got up your sleeve?*"

Dan Swain, private eye, picked up the phone and called William the Dude. He tried different numbers until he reached him out at the ranch.

"There's a problem, William," Dan said soberly. "One we can't wish away, one that is big and ugly. And it's here. Matthew Mark Judson is at the store. Timmon called and told me."

"What the hell! I guess he's really gone and done it. I heard he was up to that, but I didn't think he would go through with it," William told Dan.

He hung up and went to find Perry. He was sitting with Lily Jean Bloome and Emma near the fireplace. He tapped him on the shoulder and grinned at him.

"Perry, let's get some of that costly fruitcake I paid for to go with the hot chocolate."

Perry grinned back at him and stood up. They walked into the kitchen where the others couldn't hear their conversation. William turned to Perry.

"We got an emergency here. Against all odds, Matthew made it to the store early. You're gonna' have to go there and do something with him. Just don't bring him back here."

They went to the kitchen doorway and looked at the two thoughtful, cheerful faces gathered near the fireplace, cups of hot chocolate cradled in their hands. Perry blinked a couple times, then went silent for a minute.

"Oh hell. How do I get there, and why am I leaving?" he asked with resignation.

William told him then said, "I'll think of a big fat whopper of a lie to tell them."

He grinned at Perry.

"Don't make it too big," Perry said dryly.

÷

Perry parked the old station wagon rental beside the silver Mercedes and got out. The garage doors were open. Inside was a baby blue T-Bird with the hood up. Outside stood a tow truck. He looked at the Mercedes and sighed. Matthew's, no doubt. *May as well get it over with!*

He took the porch steps two at a time and opened the front door. He heard his father shouting something. Women's voices shouted back. He rushed through the store and into the back room and stopped.

A young man stood just inside the door. For an instant, Perry studied him. William described Timmon to him last night. Late twenties, maybe? Blond hair, tan, athletic build, blue eyes, six feet tall.

Goodness shone from him. Humor quirked at the corners of his mouth as he returned Perry's astounded look with one of calm humor.

"It's a man thing. His. Not ours. Thank God!"

He pointed at Matthew, almost in admiration. Perry's gaze shifted to the two women.

Matthew stopped shouting. He was sick and exhausted and proud of himself, for in spite of hurting so much, he'd made it to Avery's crummy little desert store to tell somebody, anybody off about the people here keeping Avery away from him. Away in a crummy little manger. He'd driven hours—or maybe days—all alone through heat and famine, only stopping at crummy little gas stations to piss and get gas. His was a hero's journey. He was convinced he was finally showing the fatherly love he'd withheld from his son. Better late than never. Since he was sick with whatever, that just made his tremendous sacrifice even greater. He'd been shouting at Timmon when the back door opened, and two women rushed in.

"What the hell's all the shouting about? Somebody wanting to kill somebody? Somebody needing an ass whipping? We're ready!" the two women shouted happily. "We'll kick your ass!" They circled Matthew.

"Who the hell are you?" he tried to shout the words, but they came out in a low growl.

"Susan Sugar Diamond and Lana Ellis. That's who the hell we are. Who the hell are you?"

"Matthew. Matthew Mark Judson."

He swayed on his feet. All thoughts of his mission and Lily Jean Bloome flew out of his head as he gazed at Lana. Sudden lust filled him. She was magnificent—wide-hipped, strong-willed. Only a man heavily experienced in wooing and with great sexual prowess need apply to this curvy, sensual woman. No skinny little rail, no wispy cutesiness. This woman was a tough, beautiful, older bloom, ready for picking. Or so he hoped. Lana stared back at him, slowly turning white as a sheet. He watched and wondered why.

She remembered him. She realized he didn't remember her. Or what happened. It happened back when she was a call girl, staying with Hal Rementen for the weekend at his home. She'd been hired to keep him happy. He was easy and actually, gentle. She spent lots of time by herself because all he wanted was for her to read to him, give him a massage and quick sex. He was on pills of some kind and slept most of the weekend while she strolled the grounds at 1228 California.

She stared at the weary stranger swaying before her and whispered, "1227 California."

He heard the whispered words and cringed.

"Your son didn't do it," she added, whispering softly.

"How do you know he didn't?" he asked hoarsely.

"Because I was staying at 1228 California that weekend."

"Who with?" he asked suspiciously. This was all happening too fast for him. It wouldn't be if he wasn't so damn hung over and exhausted. Too much scotch on the drive here. Oh well. He deserved it—any kind of narcotic to numb his pain. She looked him in the eye.

"Hal. Hal Rementen. In the house across the pond."

"Well," he growled. "What the hell is happening?"

"You're a pushy man. Used to having your own way in everything."

The women laughed as he stumbled toward Lana, reaching out his arms to embrace her. Lana sidestepped and grasped one of the man's huge arms. Susan grabbed his other arm. They tugged him toward the ugliest green sofa they'd ever seen and shoved him down onto it. He leaned back and closed his eyes.

Perry watched the two women propel his father across the back room of the store and down onto an ugly green sofa. Maybe the ugliest sofa he'd ever seen. Her name was Susan Sugar Diamond? He'd heard that name somewhere before. But where? She was his dream come true in living flesh. Luscious skin inviting touch, much more than an ample bosom to rest his head on, curves everywhere. A lush, curvy figure bordering on ridiculous. Whatever her age was, she was perfect. He knew women. Her hair was white like his underneath the blond hair color. That was good. She was old enough for him. At last. No more skinny rails or young awkward debutantes. She was a white-haired Betty Boop! He hoped she was at least a decade older than him and available.

His fascinated gaze shifted to Lana. His father was staring up at Lana like he'd finally discovered the Holy Grail. She was a bountiful, beautiful mother type with large flat hips for baby-making and carrying back in her younger years. He wondered how many children she'd borne. She was maybe a decade older than Susan Sugar Diamond? Where did he know that name from? It didn't matter to him that Susan was older. He would have fallen for her at any age.

His father was still staring at Lana. One foot on a banana peel, the other in the grave, and he was still capable of lust, Perry thought. Then he hesitated. Matthew was faithful to Dawn. And his own mother. For the first time, he realized his father's limited love capacity included a dogged faithfulness.

Perry finally realized that the two opposite beauties were studying both him and his father. He felt faint for the first time in his life. Neither one of the men realized that the women standing before them were zapping them with the powerful, holy, badass energies from the red cactus desert. They'd tanked up on those energies and were both now bold and fearless warrior women. Susan Sugar Diamond spoke first, breaking the tantalizing silence filled with all manner of possibilities surrounding them.

"Come on. It's Christmas Eve. You two are going with us. No more raising hell with these fine folks, who actually, don't seem to want any part of you right now, including your genitals!" she croaked out in a raspy voice, grinning at Timmon. He nodded in agreement. The two women looked at each other and laughed. Hands on hips, Lana studied the huge, hardened, hulk of a man with his large mane of too long white hair. He looked like a man who once ruled his world, but then got lost somehow. No doubt, he was a Leo sun sign. She shuddered. Oh, well. Once again.

"Even though the wind's been knocked out of you, you're still a fool. I'm betting it will take both me and Susan to keep you in line. And a small village," Lana chuckled.

"Yep. You're a good challenge for us. Not a great one. Just a good one."

"We're in rooms three and four. We're staying until our car is repaired. The blue T-Bird in the garage? You can have motel room three. I'll bunk in with Susan."

She glanced at Timmon. He nodded.

"Come on." She looked at Perry and waited. He crossed the room and helped them pull Matthew to his feet. He pulled Matthew's arm across his shoulder. The women took the other side of him. It took both women to handle his weighty bigness. Neither one flinched or acted girly or helpless about moving a mountain around. They were tough, Perry realized. Like beautiful, unexpected decorations you expect to be useless, but have all the get up and go of dynamos.

They stumbled across the parking lot behind the store and over to the motel. Susan, Lana, and Perry pulled the giant man through the door of motel room three, dragged him over to the bed and shoved him down on it. They stood back, heaving with relief.

"Whew!"

Perry stared at them admiringly while he caught his breath.

"Don't get any ideas, fella," Susan said to him. He realized he'd been staring, ogling, or something.

"I've been swept off my feet," Perry complained truthfully in a hoarse voice. Susan and Lana looked at each other and burst out laughing. They turned and went out the door, closing it behind them with a bang.

Perry looked at the sodden mass lying on the bed. He gently removed his father's shoes and shoved his huge bulk around until he lay mostly straight on the king size bed. Then he covered him with a blanket.

He looked around the room. It was colorful yet peaceful. Somebody knew what they were doing when they decorated this room. He shivered. He was tired. There was no choice but to stay with his father. He needed a keeper to watch over him. God knew what he would try next!

Perry turned the heater standing in a corner of the room higher. He lay down on the other side of the bed by his sleeping father. It was enough for one day.

Tomorrow is Christmas day, Perry thought as he fell asleep to dreams of Susan Sugar Diamond.

It's partly ya' doin' babe
It's partly mine
When the wind blows 'round, babe
I heah' dem' church bells chime

Part Six

Prelude to a Christmas

The sun rose slowly over the New Mexico desert, bringing the first rays of Christmas morning dawn. The air stayed windy, crisp and cold with a few snowflakes twirling their errant way down to the sand now and then. The desert store's lights were off.

The small alarm clock Cowboy Johnson always kept by his cot jangled. Timmon yawned and sat up. It was Christmas morning. Time to get up. Lots to do. Coffee to brew. A special ham to glaze and pop into the oven on low. Emma and the crew out at the ranch would be baking holiday breads and making salads. They would arrive at noon.

He rose and pulled on his jacket. The stove needed warming up and the outhouse needed tending to for the guests. Cowboy Johnson had installed a toilet in the back living quarters and one up front in a corner with a closed door for customers to use.

Hector and Annie were off for Christmas day. They'd be in tomorrow, at their insistence, not his. Timmon thought about the quiet, scented order the desert store was usually in. Those were the easy days, the easy ways. He wondered what the hell today would bring as he pulled on a jacket, drained his coffee cup, and headed to the outhouses.

A little later, Timmon dusted his hands together. Finished. The fake Christmas tree was up and in a corner ready to be decorated. The decorations were in boxes beside the tree. The ham was in the oven baking, though he wondered what other kinds of hams might be visiting the store today. Most everything he could think of was ready.

÷

Lana's thundering snores woke Susan. Groggy at first, she thought a storm was loose in the motel room. She'd been deep in sleep. She didn't remember her dreams. The wind picked up and howled around the window and door of the motel room briefly, then died down.

She sat up and yawned. It took a long-ass drive to get to this place. She wasn't complaining, though. Her thoughts flew to the beautiful, silent younger man she met, then to the older mountain of whatever the hell he was. The one that acted pole axed over Lana. She snickered as Lana snored again, then farted loudly. He should see her now.

Suddenly it dawned on her that this was Christmas morning. It was time to get up and get dressed. She laughed She'd brought along a decorated Christmas sweater just for this occasion.

Perry listened to Matthew's snoring with irritation. Matthew had kept Perry awake all night with snoring and farting. Perry sat up and glared at Matthew Mark Judson, his father, the mountain sleeping beside him in the king size bed. No more trying to sleep. Thin light poured through the window. He checked his Rolex. It was 5:30 am.

The wind howled around the door and window of the room, but the room stayed toasty warm. Perry examined the window and door with his eyes. He knew about good buildings, and this one didn't even squeak or rattle in the strong wind howling around it. Perry shivered. How cold did it get in the desert?

He'd slept in his clothes, same as Matthew. He slipped out of the motel room door, silently closing it behind him. He trudged toward the store and around it to the old station wagon to retrieve his suitcase and a travel bag out of the back. He glanced toward Matthew's Mercedes. He shrugged. Matthew was on his own.

A half an hour later, washed, shaved, dressed in jeans, a light blue long-sleeved shirt and jacket, wearing chukkas made from light leather with crepe rubber soles, Perry trudged across the parking lot and up the back steps of the store. He opened the back door and stepped in and sniffed. The most amazing smells filled the room. The coffee smelled absolutely tantalizing. A heavenly aroma vying for its place among the scents of ham—did he smell a molasses and chocolate glaze? If so, it better be baking in a 220 degree oven, nothing higher. And the ugly fake faded green Christmas tree. It needed decorations. He checked the oven. It was set at 250 degrees. He frowned and lowered it to 220. He poured himself a cup of the heavenly coffee, sipped, and set his cup on the table in the middle of the room.

He went to the brown cardboard boxes gathered around the wimpy looking fake Christmas tree and opened one. Ornaments gleamed from the box. Yes. He'd guessed right. He began to decorate the tree. He glanced at his Rolex again—it was 6:00 am. Timmon came in the back room. He grinned at Perry.

"Good morning."

He headed for the coffee pot and poured himself a cup.

"The misfits, the people that used to live here, usually come home to decorate this same tree every year at Christmas. But they couldn't get here this year because of the blizzard that's blanketing much of the country."

Perry nodded.

Timmon said, "William, Emma, and Lily Jean Bloome will arrive around noon. They're bringing lots of goodies—foods and such. Actually, God knows what else. I stay prepared for anything. Can you get that mountain of a man—Matthew—to clean up and shut up before then? William is expecting your call before they leave to come here. They've all celebrated Christmas at Cowboy Johnson's Desert Store for many years, and they want to have another good time today, especially as seeing the one they each loved so much is gone. They want any troubles set aside for today."

Timmon wiped his eyes, picked up his coffee cup, turned away and ambled back toward the front of the store.

"Got lots to do up front, even on Christmas day. We have a tradition of keeping the gas pumps open and helping anybody out for free that stops by the store today. I keep the closed sign out, but sometimes people show up anyway."

He tossed the words back over his shoulder as he left.

The back door opened. Perry turned to see who it was. Susan Sugar Diamond stood framed in the doorway, blinking at him. He gazed at her, open-mouthed. A dimpled smile and thick honey-colored, white hair, a still cute little figure, and last but not least, a wide-eyed look of complete innocence in her large blue eyes fringed with black lashes so heavy and long, he instantly wanted to hunt up a box of toothpicks and hand it to her to prop them up with. She wore a red Christmas sweater with prancing reindeer and glitter on it, black slacks, and black Mary Jane shoes.

"My, my!" he muttered, at a loss for words. She grinned at him and sashayed to the coffee pot and poured herself a cup.

"Are there any donuts or sweet rolls?" she asked in a hoarse, plaintive voice.

"I might give out unless I get some suga'."

She laughed at his expression and wandered into the front of the store. She came back carrying a box of donuts.

"I've been ordered to help you decorate the tree."

She ate a donut, drank her coffee and set her cup down.

"Now, to get to work. Christmas is my favorite time of the year!"

The strains of *Ave Maria* drifted into the back room. Timmon poked his head in. "A Christmas tradition," he said before he was gone again.

Susan hummed along with the music in her deep, hoarse voice. Perry listened and grinned to himself. He glanced at her. She was radiant, happily exuding all kinds of like, Christmas love, and a variety of flavors of love hormones with a flair. She seemed to have a vast capacity for enjoying life. He sure hoped he was reading her correctly.

The back door opened again, and Lana stepped in. Long-legged and wide-hipped in camel-colored slacks, a deceptively simple black sweater and brown loafers, she swayed, a tall solemn reed scenting the air before she gracefully removed her three quarter length coat of tan wool and laid it across a chair. She strode to the coffee pot, poured a cup and sipped.

"Ah! Heaven in a cup!" she said in a smooth, low voice.

"Get your buns over here and help us!" Susan ordered and laughed. Lana grinned.

"As soon as I get a little more heat in me. Brr! It's damn cold out there!"

Timmon came in, went to the stove and took out the ham. A wonderful fragrance of ham and chocolate filled the air and mixed with the scents of fresh coffee.

Susan, Perry, and Lana sniffed the air.

"Oh my!" they said.

"Ham. There's always a ham around somewhere in this store. Sometimes more than one," Timmon stated and grinned at them knowingly. He headed back to the front of the store, leaving them to figure out what he meant. They were laughing when the back door opened again. Matthew stumbled through the door, wrinkled clothes, reeking, unshaven, his great mane of hair standing up around his head like a misbegotten forest of wild things.

Perry, who was hanging an ornament on the tree, froze. Damn! It was maybe seven in the morning. He figured he'd have time to loiter, to bask in the presence of Susan Sugar Diamond before he'd have to deal with Matthew, who never rose until at least ten in the morning. Matthew stumbled over to the table and smashed down into a chair.

"Coffee," he ordered. Perry, Susan, and Lana ignored him.

"Coffee," he repeated. They went on decorating the tree as though he wasn't there. He slammed a meaty fist down on the table.

Susan turned around and said, "Get your own damn coffee."

"Who do you think you are? I've got more money than you'll ever have."

"I doubt that," Susan answered with hardened glee. "If you insist on measuring the world by that standard, Mr. Big Shot, my guess is it's the other way around."

Perry turned and stared at Susan in astonishment. Susan Sugar Diamond. So that's who she was! The world-famous reclusive author, worth uncounted millions because her books sold so well. She was purported to earn at least forty million a year. Susan felt his stare, turned and grinned at him.

Just then, Lana, whose back was to Matthew because she was hanging a decoration, turned around. She put her hands on her hips and looked him up and down. Matthew's eyes widened, he looked at her, then down at himself. He jumped up. All he could do was rumble from deep in his parched throat, "Imbecile!" in a tone of great anguish before he rushed out the back door, slamming it behind him. Lana snickered. Susan laughed. Perry sighed.

"Yep. That's my father. I'll have to take him a whole pot of coffee." He turned and headed for the front of the store. "I'm going to try to find out where that coffee came from and make more."

Lana and Susan turned and stared at each other.

“What the hell?” they questioned at the same time.

Matthew Mark Judson slunk hurriedly back to motel room three and slammed the door shut behind him. He slunk to the bed and sat heavily down on it. The woman was still here! She wasn’t a drunken Christmas Eve mirage like he’d convinced himself she was. He groaned. He’d gone through a whole bottle of scotch on the drive to the desert store. Christmas Eve drunk driving. He was beginning to suspect that he was guilty of that and a whole lot of other sins. Some he knew about, some were yet to come. He hoped it just wasn’t today. Why, a man that got double-crossed like he was should catch a break now and then!

He sniffed. He stunk. It was time to clean up. He looked at the primitive wash pan and the water in the pitcher. The toilet was outside in a sort of shed or something. What the hell was Avery doing, living in a place like this? What was he thinking? Judson’s didn’t live like this! They lived on a grand scale. Then he remembered, and his world crashed in on him.

“Avery’s gone?” he whispered to himself, finally admitting it at last. Thank God he was alone. He began to sob into his hands, great heaving sobs of loud remorse.

Perry skidded to a stop outside the door, holding the pot of coffee. He’d just got there when he heard Matthew start bellowing. He decided not to go in. Matthew needed to get through this on his own or he’d never grow up. He was responsible for all of it.

Perry clenched his jaw and turned grimly away. He trudged back to the store and set the pot down on the stove, planted his hands on the counter and stared straight ahead.

"You all right, suga'?" Susan questioned.

"Strangely enough, I don't seem to be at the moment. Raising a father is hard work."

Susan went to him and put a hand on his arm.

"Come sit down," she said. She led him to the table.

"Where is he—your father? Is he okay?" Lana asked. Perry shrugged and sighed. His hands were shaking.

"He's crying over Avery—at last. Avery was my only brother, my only family," he explained. "He owned this store. People around here knew him as Cowboy Johnson."

He put his head in his hands. Timmon stood in the doorway watching, exuding comfort and Light. Susan made soft cooing sounds and embraced him. He leaned his head against her and sighed with relief.

"We never really had a mother," he said. "She left me and Avery when we were small boys. She left Matthew, went to Europe and married that damn duke. We haven't seen or heard from her since. She doesn't give a damn about us—oh God, I mean only me now!"

Lana's eyes met Timmon's. They were misted with tears. He went to the coffee pot and said firmly to

Lana, "Take him to his father. They need each other right now. Finally. Help her," he ordered Susan.

Lana led the way across the parking lot to the motel room, gripping the coffee pot like it was the Holy Grail. Susan and Perry trailed behind her with Susan half holding the devastated Perry up. Lana twisted the doorknob with one hand and shoved the door open with a hip.

Matthew looked up from where he sat on the bed. Lana stared at him. He was a broken-down mess. Susan untangled Perry's death grip on her and shoved him through the motel room door. He stumbled toward Matthew as Lana set the coffee pot down. He stopped, and Susan shoved him towards Matthew again. Lana pulled on Matthew until he stood up. She shoved him forward toward Perry. They met and embraced in their grief. Mindless men now, they began howling and shouting and crying for the lost brother and son they'd both neglected. Susan and Lana heard Matthew say, "I've been afraid to say I love you to anybody my whole damn life," Perry answered, "I'm afraid I'll never be able to say that to anyone my whole life."

Susan and Lana hastily backed out the door and slammed it shut behind them. They thought about locking it at the same time.

"Nah," they both said.

"Great minds think alike," Susan said smugly.

They laughed shakily and moseyed back to the store with arms linked. Somebody needed to carry on. The two powerful moguls that ran boardrooms all over the world were reduced to small boys for now. Though they were mightily attracted to them, the men were out of order for the time being. Busy doing other things. Susan and Lana suspected, for the first time.

"That deal is sort of like re-claiming a son and a father on Christmas day. Isn't that sort of holy and smarmy religious? I think I'll use it in my next book," Susan said to Lana. They both laughed. "Well, it couldn't happen to them on a better day. Lord, help us! Who knows what might happen next today? Hell, I may gather up a bunch of Christmas stories before it ends. Let's get that tree done and sample that amazing smelling ham before anything else happens."

They hurried through the back door. Timmon was calmly decorating the tree as though two grown men breaking down in a motel room at the desert store was common fare. Lana narrowed her eyes and looked around. The air was heavy with energy. A long time ago, this place and the people living here had changed her life for the better. Wasn't that why she was back here on Christmas day? At these crossroads? Maybe to return the favor to someone? This was a sacred place. A crossroads to better decisions. She just knew it. Susan and Lana turned to the Christmas tree. Timmon went to the stove and examined the ham.

"It needs to rest," he explained. Then to Susan, "Nice to smell Rose in Winter perfume. It's quite new. Is it yours?"

Susan was speechless. She nodded. Her hands were shaking. She dropped an ornament.

"Here now. We can't have all the ornaments broken," he smiled. "You ladies take this box of gifts and drive out to the red cactus desert and tarry a bit until you feel better, okay? This is Christmas Day, and these are their presents. We've been saving presents up for them. We take them to them each year. Here's a thermos of hot coffee to take with you."

He handed Susan the thermos and Lana a box filled with rusty tin cans, an old tin water bucket with a hole in it, and other junk.

"How did you know we'd been there?"

*

Finally! The store was empty. At least for a few minutes, Timmon hoped. He took a deep breath. At least part of it was over. More to come. He went to the phone and called William.

"Perry and Matthew are in motel room three bawling their eyes out over Avery. Susan Sugar Diamond and Lana Ellis are out at the red cactus desert, shooting them up and delivering presents to the cacti. It's time for Lily Jean Bloome's magic."

William said, "Well, dog my cats!... Okay." He hung up.

A short time later, William ambled into the store, followed by Lily Jean Bloome. Timmon strode past William and threw his arms around her. They hugged while William pushed his crumpled western straw hat back on his head and watched. They parted. She sighed.

"Good work, Timmon!" she said. "You've done enough on your own. Now you need help. We're here. We'll take some of it over now."

"Damn glad of it, too!" Timmon ambled toward the back room. "I might just get a chance to finish my cooking and Christmas preparations now while Emma is putting the finishing touches on the ranch food."

William smiled at Timmon. He was absurdly proud of him and the way he retained his equanimity in the face of every kind of adversity. He sometimes forgot that Timmon carried the Sight, too, inherited it from his wicked mother. But Timmon's Sight was filled with Goodness. Always would be.

Lily Jean Bloome and William went through the store and out the back. They opened the door to motel room number three, joined hands, stepped in and closed the door behind them. Perry was sitting beside Matthew on the bed. Matthew looked at William and Lily Jean Bloome. He nodded.

"I don't know how you got here or why, but I'm damned okay with it."

William examined Matthew's sodden, crumpled face.

"I see ya' been havin' a cry, Matthew. Maybe over Avery?"

Matthew growled. Perry nodded and spoke for both of them.

"Yes. Both of us. We're so damn sorry!"

He dropped his head.

"Anything else ya' want ta' say? Now's the time."

William would not and could not give Matthew Mark Judson an inch. He could Perry, but not much. Not right now when his heart was angrier than ever over their lifelong neglect and ill-treatment of Avery. Lily Jean Bloome interrupted William's buildup.

"It's time for you to go back to the ranch and collect Emma and the food for the Christmas dinner, remember? I'll handle this. Timmon can do the rest," she said to him.

William turned on his heel and left. He moseyed across the parking lot and into the back of the store where Timmon was working on something near the stove. Timmon took one look at William's face and said, "Here. Try this." He slapped a plate filled with steaming mac and cheese down in front of William. He knew William couldn't resist mac and cheese. Anytime, anywhere. William picked up a fork.

÷

Lily Jean Bloome dragged a chair across the room and positioned it close to the two men sitting on the bed. She took her seat in the chair while they watched silently as though they'd been called to appear before a judge. She gathered the strength a wise woman owns and filled her Being with Light and love. Then she spoke sternly in a voice that brooked no argument whatsoever. No court of appeals in her jurisdiction.

"Okay. First of all, Perry, you are excused. For good from this situation. Permanently. Do you understand? You are forgiven by the beloveds, the Angels, by the Creator, and absolved. You've taken on this man's responsibilities for him long enough. It is over. The situation Matthew Mark Judson created with Avery Mott Judson was not of your making and is no longer your responsibility to handle. That responsibility and all it entails reverts back to him as of this very moment, so that both of you may abide within the Laws of Karma. It is Matthew's Karma to handle it starting this very moment. All will be done forthwith in the highest good of all."

She made a sign with her hand.

"Perry Judson, you've come full circle with what you've owed this rebellious, irresponsible soul sitting here named Matthew Mark Judson. The debt is paid in full. You've been his son many times and because of it, done without the love you've needed. She awaits your return at the store. You two are free to go on adventures, there will be children brought to you to care for, and love to make work in many ways. Get cleaned up and go to her."

Perry stood. For some reason, his heart didn't hurt anymore. His tears had somehow dried up inside and out without him knowing it. He was done with them. Tenderness filled his heart and echoed hallelujah in his soul. Lily Jean Bloome was right. He'd born the burdens of his shouting, ranting father his whole life. He'd worked with the bad situations his father caused and bettered them when he could, stayed out of the ones he couldn't, and been a good son. His chest swelled with delight. Now he could go be his own man? Well, strike while the iron was hot! Susan Sugar Diamond was waiting for him in the store!

Always fastidious, he moved through the room swiftly, changing his soggy, wet shirt and grooming himself, his soul expanding as he kept one ear open, listening to Lily Jean Bloome raking his father over the coals. He hoped she whipped the hell out of him with her words. He smirked, free as a young boy. Matthew sat like a sodden hulk on the bed, mutely accepting her scolding. Lily Jean Bloome never took her eyes off him.

"You are mostly to blame, as you usually are, but not all. There's much more, but not today. Today, it's just you and Perry. You abdicated your responsibilities to him from the start and piled your obligations to others on him. You left him to take care of and nourish any love that bloomed in your family generations. Your wife—his mother—left because of your roaring, rage-filled emptiness. She was a match for you with it, but two rages can't exist together. They would have destroyed both of you, or one of you would have been healed. You knew it would be her, but you wouldn't make the sacrifice for her. It was you getting it or nothing.

She left, so it became Perry's turn. You unloaded it all on him and played out being the tyrant without caring one iota about what was happening to him. He survived you though, and became tempered steel and placed his yearning for a true love in a cage and locked the door to keep it safe. He did that because of a past life debt he owed to you that needed to be paid. You never earned his loyalty. He owed it. There's a major difference in those two things! You carry a dumb madness in your soul that refuses to learn. I only hope Lana can help you to let it go."

Perry was clean and dressed. He felt wonderful. Maybe he could finally have what he needed. He shrugged into his jacket. Fresh and dapper again, carrying changes within that were still going on, he slipped out the door of motel room number three at the desert store. He heard Lily Jean Bloome's words to Matthew just before he shut the door.

"You're a lucky prick. You didn't get to this desert store on your own. Avery somehow brought you here. Now get your ass off that bed, clean yourself up, and get dressed. Come over to the store when you're decent. Plan to mind your manners. It's time for you to finally meet your match."

Perry waited outside for Lily Jean Bloome to come out. When she did, together, arm in arm, in total agreement, they sauntered across the parking lot and went in the back door.

÷

It was eleven o'clock. William was out at the ranch gathering the food and Emma for the trip back to the desert store to celebrate Christmas day. They would eat together and whatever happened after that would happen. Not before Christmas dinner, though. They would break bread together in peace.

Emma was quietly efficient, retaining her equanimity. *Maybe it would be a good Christmas after all, though an odd one for sure,* William thought. *Well, what could be expected but the Fates to intervene any old damn way they chose? The word odd wasn't in their vocabulary. Along with good riddance, goodbye, and hark, you again? No, they chose from whatever slices of the souls of people's past lives they wanted to, spliced them together in this lifetime time frame, then sat back to watch what happened like it was a damn movie!*

"Dog my cats!" he thought. They left for the store.

÷

"I could use some help with the table and a few other things," Timmon said.

Susan and Perry ignored him. They stood by the tree, forgotten ornaments in their hands, glazed eyes fastened on each other. They were murmuring. Lana was watching Susan murmur. She didn't know Susan could murmur.

"I'll help." Lana set her coffee cup down and stood.

"Well, Cowboy Johnson, known to you by now as Avery, stored things in that closet next to the cot. Dishes and things. There's a set of Christmas dishes and other stuff somewhere in there."

Timmon pointed past the cot. Lana eyed the dresser standing between the closet and the army cot. There were cherubs and angels holding various battle equipment posed in strategic locations around the edge of the top of the dresser, as though they were protecting both the closet and the cot. Lana grinned and opened the closet door.

At 11:20 a.m., the back door of the store opened to admit Matthew Mark Judson into the festivities. He was clean and presentable in a white shirt, charcoal gray slacks, and shiny, very large black shoes. Everyone ignored him except Lana. She stopped arranging Christmas plates on the table and stared fixedly at him. He stared back. Suddenly Lily Jean Bloome stood close to her.

"Watch out! Your lower chakras are responding to that foolish man. Keep them covered. Gird your loins, girl. It's just an inch at a time with stubborn asshole souls like his," She murmured to Lana. "Too much fire element. Too haughty from pride. Pride caused by too much fire. Fire rules the soul, you know. Lots of other crap going on there too. Beware."

She turned and walked away. Lana stared after her.

Who the hell was she? Some kind of Seer or prophet? Lana wanted him. It was plain and simple. To hell with chakras or whatever. She wanted him more than any man she'd ever seen. She stared at Matthew and forgot all about Lily Jean Bloome. The hum grew louder. Suddenly, Lana fled into a past life where she knew all about Matthew Mark Judson.

He'd been her secret. She'd rescued him. She'd been placed near him to see the truth about Avery and more and to deliver it to him this lifetime.

So, that's what it was! I've always reacted with my loins when it comes to him. I've been missing this soul terribly, she thought. *How about that? But we could never stay together. We parted each time to keep from destroying each other. We were hell-bent on loving each other to death each time we got together. We had as great a need to do that as we did to have sex. We couldn't keep our hands off of each other. But sadly, we both became more accident-prone the closer we got to each other. Goddamned Karma! Who the hell knew? Us getting together was like chopped Spam and hard fried eggs being slapped together on a sizzling platter, it was like lightning striking a thunder cloud, and instead of the damn electric hitting the ground, it just reached up into our heads and blanked out all thoughts of where we were and what danger we might be in. We failed at the roulette we played, and it killed us each lifetime.*

Lana shuddered.

Still, she wanted him. Intensely. He wanted her too. They stared at each other. Suddenly, Lily Jean Bloome stood beside her again. She spoke sternly.

"Do not allow him to lower your energy in this sacred place like he has done to you in many past lifetimes. You have the opportunity right now to stop lifetimes of your abuse of each other. You're calling it accidents; well, it wasn't. Do it. It is a gift from the holy place you are standing in, if you want it. His soul has a reckoning coming today and more days, and you are only one small part of it. So chill your loins, girl. Love doesn't need you to express for it. Get out of its way like you never did before. Mind your own business. Which you're not very good at, by the way. Practice. It will make you perfect someday."

Lily Jean Bloome walked away.

Susan was watching Lana. The attraction between Lana and Matthew Mark Judson was intense. *Lana, once again, had found something she wanted—something that wasn't good for her. She remembered how Lana always and forever stuck out that strong jaw of hers and surged forward whenever questionable things went on around them back at the orphanage. Her inner being carried a light that shined in the darkest of evil corners. She kept her rage turned on day and night. After too many years of watching out for herself and me, her light never went off, and she became a savage of immense proportions when crossed.*

Lana was an immense beauty, too. A maiden fair, a wonder to behold, beautiful physically, and bold. She had wide hips and a flat belly, a gorgeous, ravishing smile, and a low chuckle instead of a laugh. She smiled all the time, even in her sleep. But it was a grim smile. She is a warrior princess of the highest order. I let her protect and cherish me back in the orphanage days, but I didn't carry her internal rage. That's what causes her to want to screw left and right, indiscriminately. Obsessions.

Lana stood by me as best she could back then, though she was damaged just as much as the rest of us. She curled my hair and instructed me that looking pretty in the world was the way to get out of the orphanage and get ahead in life.

She ran away and left me when she was seventeen and I was seven. By then, she'd taught me how to walk and laugh and talk to men and take care of Teddy. She left Teddy in my care when she ran away. Eyes sparkling, she told me, "I'll be back to get him—and you—as soon as we set up housekeeping. He has a good steady job, and has promised to adopt Teddy."

She grabbed my hands and whirled me in a circle that day. But Lana's plans for Teddy didn't work out. She couldn't make a home for him. She married a man so handsome he stopped the moon in its tracks, as she put it. He promised to adopt Teddy, but he wouldn't. He said he wanted his own "blood" children, not some ailing sickling. For a while, Lana stayed beautiful and proud and ran her silent, childless (on purpose-her secret) home with an iron fist. But she stayed in insistent denial of who he was. That was always her downfall.

Lana still processes life in terms of good or bad, black and white, and she always needed to be good. That's why she carries a gun. She assumes that everyone else is either all good or all bad. There was no gray for Lana. Just black and white. You couldn't be both and exist in her world.

She ignored me for a decade or so when she thought of me as "Bad," then she called one day, and I was "Good" again. Who knows why? That was after she'd kicked her husband out and started seeing other men. Her only husband turned out to be a gambling, conniving hot head. She left him after many faithful times of looking the other way over his women and his slaps. She always picked disgusting men. She never learned! Susan thought.

Susan glared at Matthew Mark Judson, her sky blue eyes filled with a cold frost that would have frozen a smart person to death. But the big fool never noticed, he just stared at Lana. *Damn their internal righteous rage!* She glared at Lana and whistled. Lana whirled around. Susan's eyes were piercing as they stared into hers. There was a hum in the air. Susan's eyes seemed to be saying, don't make the same mistake twice!

Suddenly, Perry stood beside her. He shook his head.

"That's my father."

Susan looked at him, emotions running across her face.

"They're both old. Maybe that will help," Perry said.

"Well, we are... mature, too!"

"Yeah, we are. But not as old as them!" he laughed.

"Well," she finally said, "I sure as hell hope you're not the asshole he is."

"I sure as hell hope not, too," Perry answered.

Heah' comes da' pacin' of da' beatin' hearts
dat' belongs to dis' place
an' dis' time
ta' partake a' dis' season a' peace

Part Seven

They heard voices in the front of the store. The voices and laughter came closer. Matthew's eyes moved from Lana to the tiny woman in front of William. She was holding a huge basket of bread or something. Matthew blinked. She looked liked one of the fairy women in his childhood books, Minus the wings. He snorted. Lana put her hands on her hips and glared at him.

"I'm Emma," the tiny, svelte woman said. He froze a couple seconds then looked down at his coffee cup. He picked it up and took a sip and set it down hastily. He frowned. His coffee was cold. How did that happen? Was he staring at Lana that long?

The woman spoke again. He stared at her open-mouthed. In the few seconds he'd sipped his coffee and discovered it was cold, some kind of Light was starting to blossom around her. Odd. William and Lily Jean Bloome stood on each side of her. Matthew and Perry stared at Lily Jean Bloome and Emma. They'd gained a startling, beautiful Light in just a short time. Helpless before them, startled out of their usual assumptions concerning women, thrown into awe, Perry unconsciously moved backward step by step until he stood by Matthew's chair.

Emma and Lily Jean Bloome eyed Avery's kin. One old, mangy father and his dapper and distant neglectful brother. Both who never grew up. The women glanced at each other in agreement. No wonder Avery bought the little church and turned it into a desert store hideout for himself!

It was obvious that Avery's current male generations didn't understand women or life in its bigger aspects, as Avery had learned to do. These men didn't realize they were so guarded against women that their lives stayed bereft of the humanity a loving woman brings to it. Avery had discovered that secret early on, and it had saved him.

Matthew Mark Judson either bullied and shouted his way through life or self-sacrificed himself to a sickening, demeaning extreme. Perry Mott Judson owned a better grip, a better philosophy on life, but his was estranged from intimate companionship. He never let any woman search out his soul and touch it with her warmth and magic.

They shuddered. Avery had somehow brought his womanless father and brother together at his place, this desert store, against all odds on their first Christmas without him in this world.

The women glared at the men. What the hell to do with them? Neither of them were anything like Avery. Neither bore his limitless capacity for kindness, common sense, compassion, observation, gentleness, equanimity, handsomeness...

Timmon interrupted their train of thought.

"Before you turn you-know-who into a saint," he grinned at them, young, blond, tan, and with the Sight he inherited from his mother.

"William, want to help me bake a cherry pie?"

"No way," William said.

"Just do it!" the women hissed. "Now!"

William blanched as their combined energies hit him. He shrugged and joined Timmon at the kitchen sink. The two men kept their backs turned to the events going on in the room as if baking a cherry pie was all that existed in the world.

The women glanced at each other. *Smart boys*, they thought.

Matthew stared at the men, his eyebrows raised, then back at the women as if to say, "You can't make men mind like that! Don't try it on me!"

The battle between their combined Sight and Matthew was beginning. But first, Perry needed to get the hell out of the way. He would not be allowed to protect his spoiled and selfish father anymore. Emma gave him an order.

"Perry, brother of Avery, take Susan and go find appropriate Christmas music to play on Cowboy Johnson's Victrola in the front of the store. It was a tradition he always kept. There are many albums in the cupboard below the Victrola. Take your time, look through them, and play whatever comes to you that Avery would have liked."

Perry nodded. Susan took his arm and led him from his protective stance by Matthew. Susan smiled at Lily Jean Bloome and Emma.

"Ah'm guessin' Matthew has to go it alone?"

The women shook their heads.

"For the moment. Perry, we'll want you back in here shortly."

Susan chuckled and nodded happily as they grabbed the astonished Lana and swept her out of the room with them.

"Yeah!"

William and Timmon dropped what they were doing and headed to the front of the store.

"Better you before the firing squad than me!" He drawled happily to Matthew. Matthew huffed at him then stared at the two women again. He decided to engage the women first. Intimidate and surprise them, something he knew how to do very well.

"What the hell's going on? You're not going to stop me from taking this place over! It belonged to my son! I have the right!" Matthew thundered.

"No, you don't," Emma said. "You forfeited your right to any part of Avery Mott Judson's life when he was ten years old and before."

Lily Jean Bloome chimed in. "You have no rights. This is the second and last time I will tell you who you are and how to leave this place a different person than you were when you came here with your nonsense about grief and love and rights. If you don't get it this time, then you're done. I can't help you."

In a steely, whispery voice, Emma said, "You're cruel, and you're violent. And you like it. Power. Shall I show you some power?"

Matthew snarled. "Sure. Go ahead, if you think you can."

A gust of wind shook the back door. Matthew jumped. He decided to take a different tack.

"What the hell was that? Look, I only came here to tell Avery how sorry I am. What's wrong with that?"

"No, you didn't. You came to take away and hoard all that Avery left behind for his beloveds, the people who earned it. We won't let you do that. This property is not for sale for any price of any kind. Not one square inch of it.

"I don't think you realize this is a sacred place, a healing Earth chakra. That Avery lived a sacred life in this sacred place. A little church that became a gas station and grocery store with a garage and later, a motel and restaurant added on. But it stayed a church with over a hundred years of healing energies still steeped in its boards and bones. Many people stopped here and were healed. Many unusual people have come here, causing healing events to take place, to the good of all.

The misfits that lived here were accepted and healed. In this desert, this place of drought and space, Avery made a spiritual rest stop for the wounded healers of this world that were passing through.

You don't fit that category. You don't know yourself well enough. Avery brought two generations, his brother, and father together here at his special place for Christmas. We don't want you here. Only he does," Emma said.

"We wouldn't let you be here, but it looks like he's still running the show... He brought you here...Somehow," Lily Jean Bloome said grudgingly.

"Quit hemming and hawing. I'm going to give them their gifts from Avery. It's the only chance they've got," Emma interrupted.

From somewhere, she produced two brown wrapped 8x10 packages. "They were in the closet." She said bitterly, nodding toward the closet door by Cowboy Johnson's cot.

"Perry, come in here and go to your father. You'll both have to come and get them. I won't take one step to bring them to you in protest of the way you both treated Cowboy Johnson when he was alive."

Perry came in and went to Matthew. Matthew jumped up and strode over to Emma. She handed him his package. He grabbed it without a thank you and strode back to the table. He sat down and ripped the brown wrapper off while Perry walked slowly over to Emma. She handed him his package.

"This is yours by law, but not by like," she said.

Perry shuddered and bowed his head as he turned away and walked back toward Matthew. She watched him.

"No, Perry. Will you never learn? Take your gift, Perry, into the other room, not to your father! You two cannot share this, for your souls are on different evolutionary paths!"

Matthew ignored them as he stared down into Avery's steady, cool green eyes. His heart started breaking at the sight of his handsome, grown up son. He saw the Light glowing in his son and felt the Goodness his son had attained. All without the benefit of a good father. Him. Maybe it was supposed to be that way. Maybe Avery couldn't have attained the character development Matthew saw in the picture with a lower life form like him around. Oh, how he wished it wasn't true! But it was.

The hard-hearted ways Matthew's soul stubbornly nourished all his life were astounded. They fell away from him like drops of rain. He couldn't steel his heart against his son's steadfast gaze. A faint, pink, new blossoming of wonder began in his soul. Ornery, old, complacent sins were astonished at the newcomer and began packing up, planning to flee.

"Thank you, my beautiful son. I don't deserve your forgiveness," he finally whispered.

Perry sat down on the floor. Susan knelt beside him. He began chanting the Lord's Prayer as he gently removed the brown paper wrapping. He looked down into Avery's loving, steady silver-green eyes, and his heart broke with the love he'd held back from him. Avery was not his father. Just his only beloved brother. Not someone he should have held his love and caring back from. Suddenly, he hated Matthew. He began recounting all the bad he'd done to him and Avery. Suddenly, it felt like a hand swiped over his forehead, and he could hear clearly and was unburdened.

"You are no longer your brother's keeper. Or your father's." He heard Cowboy Johnson's words in his head. "Stay away from Matthew until you can forgive him. I did."

He felt a gentle touch on his arm. He looked up. It was Susan. Her face was wet with tears for him. Lana edged near, trying to see the picture.

"No. Go see Matthew's picture," Susan said, shielding Perry's picture from Lana.

Lana went to Matthew. He showed her the picture.

"Did you know him?"

Lana gasped and her hand flew to her mouth.

"Oh my God! It's the man I almost shot who turned out to be an angel! Did he die?"

She looked at the picture again.

"Oh my God! It's the beautiful, innocent boy I saw at 1227 California! I saw the same boy after he was grown and almost shot him! But he and a girl, about thirteen she was way back then, sent me to the red cactus desert, and I shot it up, and it saved my soul, and I went home different. Those two angels saved my life and set me on a different path. I'm so sorry!"

She burst into tears.

"For God's sake, Matthew!" Lily Jean Bloome shouted. "Get off your stupid ass and take care of Lana! She's got some kind of Karma going on about your son, she's encountered him twice in truth, which is more than you have, but evidently, you think you're all there is in the world!"

Matthew shoved himself to his feet and went to Lana.

"What do I do?" he asked.

Lily Jean Bloome started to answer, but William interrupted her.

"Matthew, do what you've never done before. Be kind to a woman. Take her in your arms and hold her. Give her comfort, not sexual energy."

Matthew swept Lana into his massive arms, but it wasn't enough. He swept her off her feet like she was a feather, carried her to the ugly green sofa and sat down with her in his arms.

By then, Perry and Susan were standing in the backroom doorway.

"I can't stand this," Perry exclaimed.

"Well, suga', let's go for a walk. Get a breath of fresh air in us."

Perry laid his picture on the store counter, rushed Susan into her coat and slammed into his.

"Let's get the hell out of here! I don't care if it's forty below out there!"

"Me neither," Susan said.

Perry didn't know Susan was a snow bunny who loved Arctic temperatures. But Lana knew. The two women exchanged quick looks.

Later that evening, just after dark set in, after all was said and done, and the Christmas meal reheated and eaten, William went to the front of the store and came back carrying a sheaf of papers in Cowboy Johnson's handwriting.

He began leafing through them.

"What ya' got there, William?" Lily Jean Bloome asked. Everyone waited for his answer.

"This is one of Cowboy Johnson's tall tales. He liked to write short stories, especially about birds...But this one is about something else...a coyote, maybe? I haven't read it yet. You see, Mama left it with instructions for me to hide it and read it on Christmas evening. Do you want to hear it? It will be sort of like having Avery here with us for Christmas, but knowing him, I'm warning you that only God knows what kind of story it is."

"Oh, yes!" Susan, Emma, Lily Jean Bloome, Perry, Timmon, Matthew, and Lana chorused, laughing. Quickly, they settled themselves here and there. Perry held Susan's small, curvy hand in his large, sturdy one. Timmon and Lily Jean Bloome pulled up chairs together. Lana pushed Matthew down into a large chair at the kitchen table and stood behind him, leaning on him, hands on his shoulders. Emma sat next to William on the ugly green sofa.

William stared at the first piece of paper. Finally he read the few words on it to them.

"It says here, 'This is a story for the new and the old eight. Unless someone else shows up, too."

"Well, dog my cats!" he muttered. "How did he know there would be eight of us...like there was back in the beginning..."

A look of wonder stole over his face before he began to read.

"Once upon a time there was a cobbler who plied his trade in the back room of a general store. He particularly liked the pickles they sold in the front of the store and often bought one to eat for lunch. He ate while he worked, which meant pickle juice sometimes fell on the shoes he repaired. The pickle juice combined with the smell of old, mostly worn out leather carried a very distinct, but pleasant smell.

Now you may think that has nothing to do with this story, but pickle juices always choose one of two paths. They invariably pickle things or put things in a pickle. Even a small amount of pickle juice will do it. Just one single drop can start a cycle of circumlocution. The more fragrant the pickles are, the more paraphrasing gets done.

Now, concerning other pertinent facts, a father, a son, and a grandson ran the general store, which was built back in the father's grandfather's day. So there were many generations concerned and involved with the running of the store, especially at Christmas. This was because of their Knowledge Degrees. Each year at Christmas, the three living generations, sometimes with help from the non-living generations, vied for the academic equivalent of a Ph.D. in Knowing IT All. Each generation was markedly different from the other and didn't like their differences. They all wanted each other to be exactly as they were. But as life would have it, even in the most stubborn of species, each generation always stays a little different from the next.

Well, the father shouted and paced and stirred the air with furious Exclamations. The son traveled over hills and dales to keep away from the father's furious Exclamations. To explain his absences, he kept Long Lists and traveled everywhere seeking bargains to sell in the store. The Beautiful grandson swaggered about, dressed in the finest of clothes, ignored everyone else, and spent his time admiring himself in the many mirrors he placed here and there in the store. He would have swaggered about elsewhere, but he had to make a living, and the store was it. In fact, the store was the inherited heritage of all three men.

The three generations did what they did, while the pickle loving cobbler stayed quiet and steady, doing his cobbling work in the back room. The cobbler turned out handsome, well-made, pickle scented repaired boots and re-soled shoes, which gave their weary wearers a better understanding of life, something they never noticed, but enjoyed nonetheless.

Another thing they didn't notice was that each year at Christmas, their feet fairly danced about their work while they wore the shoes repaired by the cobbler. They became happy and much less tired than they would have been otherwise. The cobbler knew he was doing a good behind-the-scenes service, and he was satisfied for a while.

More Christmases went by. People danced in his cobbled shoes. He looked out the window and watched the falling sand or snow, whatever they danced through, but nobody noticed him or gave him credit for his work or said, "Hi," to him.

Inevitably, though the cobbler was happy, in time, he grew lonesome. He yearned for something that wasn't a part of his life yet, so he closed up shop, filled a knapsack, and went out in search of it. Meanwhile, the three generations of men in the front of the general store never noticed he was gone, they were so busy tending to who they thought they were—business, as usual.

Then things changed. One day, a coyote wandered into the empty store. The three men were busy doing other things like accounting, sweeping the back porch, and changing the oil in a car. The coyote was skinny and pitiful looking. It wandered around, sniffing everything until it came to the open pickle barrel. It sniffed the pickle barrel, sat down on its hind legs, peed, and began to howl.

The three men heard it and ran into the store. They tried to shoo the coyote out, but it wouldn't budge from its spot by the pickle barrel. Every few minutes, the coyote quit howling and sniffed the pickle barrel. Then it went back to peeing and howling again. Well, nobody knew what to do. The few customers that came in the store gave the father, son, and grandson what they thought to be sage advice.

Shoot it.

Throw something at it.

Things like that. Well, though the father, son, and grandson thought they were of the temperament it took to kill the coyote, they weren't. None of them could do it, nor could they let anyone else do it. So, the coyote sat by the pickle barrel and just kept on peeing and howling. Night fell. A full Moon rose above and behind the store. The coyote peed and howled louder than ever in between bouts of pickle smelling. Coyotes always pee more and howl louder during the full Moon, you see, because they own, as a genetic right of the dog and wolf species, proprietary rights to the Moon's full ascendancy.

Well, the father couldn't scuff around in his house slippers, comfortably shouting. He couldn't hear himself. Or listen to his own advice. Or to the important gurgles and rumbles of his innards.

The son couldn't meditate on numbers or mediate with his father and others, which was actually his strong suit. Remorsefully, he realized he should have trained as a lawyer. It might have been very profitable.

The grandson couldn't leave for imaginary places in his mind where young women smiled at his astounding beauty and embraced him.

The grandson watched the coyote with contempt at first. He had an eye for beauty, he told himself. This was the ugliest coyote he'd ever seen. But the more he watched, the less he fussed about himself and the more beautiful the coyote became. Before long, he saw the beauty that lies within reality in the coyote's skinny body. He saw the coyote's beautiful life force thriving, strumming away, peeing and howling away on just a little pickle juice. Suddenly he realized he'd lived on the surface of life. How deep was it? Deeper than he'd ever thought. What was down below? Beneath the fur and skin and bone? He could almost hear something. He kept studying the coyote.

One day, his grandfather came in, holding a shotgun. He was shouting. Nothing new in that. He aimed the shotgun at the coyote, but his grandson jumped between them.

"No!" he shouted. "You will not do this! The coyote is beautiful and he is entitled to his beauty. Let him live!"

The shouting grandfather lowered his gun and called out to his son.

"Come in here and settle this!" (in my favor, as usual, was what he meant.)

The son paced into the room and all around it while the grandfather and grandson watched and waited. The son decoded and deducted and finally handed the father a piece of paper. On it were written the words, “The cobbler must be dead.”

“What cobbler?” the father shouted.

“The one that works in the backroom,” the son answered.

“Oh, him,” the father said.

The grandson didn’t hear them. He was watching the coyote become paler and sort of luminous. Soon, he could see the bones inside the coyote. Did he have x-ray vision? He’d always suspected he did, for he was special. The grandfather shouted rudely to the coyote.

“What do you want from me? For I have nothing to give except shouting.”

He glared at his son and grandson.

“And that is all their fault.”

The coyote didn’t answer. It just glimmered away.

The son and grandson stared at the father. The father stared back at them. Just at that instant, they heard someone whistling. Then the cobbler walked through the front door. He whistled for the coyote to follow him as he walked past them and into the back room. The coyote followed him. They both smelled strongly of pickles. Dill or maybe...bread and butter?

The three men heard the cobbler’s footsteps echoing through the back room. Then they heard the back door close. The three generations of men, father, son, and grandson stared at each other.

“He’s gone for good. Oh no!” they said, all at the same time. This was their first agreement on anything.

The grandfather whispered his words mournfully, for he knew what was coming. Suddenly he knew he'd live in sorrow until the cobbler came back. And the cobbler wasn't coming back. Oh, well, he decided. He would just keep shouting instead of mending his fences. It was easier. The price was less. He hurried to add vinegar to make the pickle juice stronger. He sniffed the air. The pickle scent grew stronger, beckoning him. He followed the scent of it out the back door and toward the forest, shouting in between sniffs.

The son pictured taming wild horses, and the lion his father was forever. The idea of that project going on forever exhausted him. He decided he would deduce some more deductions with a view toward finding the proper path he should take along with purchasing a pair of earplugs. Why didn't he think of earplugs before? A simply sensible remedy! He added more pickles to the pickle barrel to ferment before he hurried out the back door toward the forest.

The grandson smoothed his shirtfront and sighed. He'd seen the innards, the bones of the coyote, a living being, exposed to him in all of its terrible beauty. He would seek more beauty out in the world, that's all it meant, he decided. And he would go find it. He was hungry. Was it time to eat yet? He casually tossed in a large scoop of pickling spices into the pickle barrel before he made himself a sandwich and strolled out the back door of the general store.

And so, the father shouted, and the son put in his new earplugs, and the grandson ate while they all followed the cobbler, who was rambling through the nearby forest with the coyote in search of new shoes to repair or re-sole.

The End

William handed the sheets of paper to Emma.

"Well, dog my cats! I guess only Mama knows what that story means. And she's gone." He got up to fix himself a cup of coffee and grab a slice of fruitcake. Silence filled the store. They heard an engine start up and leave. The sound died away. They looked at each other. No one got up to see who it was. Perry squeezed Susan's hand. Timmon headed for the front of the store. Lana went to the coffee pot and poured her and Matthew cups of coffee. She carried them to the table and sat down beside him. He glanced at her and picked up his cup with a giant paw.

"Wonder if there's any donuts left?" he asked raggedly. Lana sighed and rolled her eyes heavenward. Emma and William went to the Christmas tree and began to rearrange ornaments. Susan grinned at Perry. She stood and went to Lana and Matthew, who were staring at each other again.

"Come on, Lana. We need to talk."

Lana reluctantly tore her gaze away from Matthew's and followed Susan out onto the back porch. Susan closed the door and got right to the point.

"Are we taking them home with us?"

"They're not pets, Susan. Maybe they won't want to. They're men. Smelly, hairy fools living close to the cave so they can run back in and revert to Neanderthals when needed." Lana said. "Besides, we haven't done anything like that in a long time. It's a big chance to take."

"Well, I think it's time to take another chance. There you have it. Wanna' bet on who wins?" Susan smirked.

After a long moment, Lana said, "Okay. Let's do it."

Late that night, when Cowboy Johnson's Desert Store, once upon a time a little white church, was empty, and all the lights were out in the motel rooms across the parking lot, the wind picked up sand and covered the place where Cowboy Johnson once sat at the campfire.

÷

Timmon tossed and turned on Cowboy Johnson's cot in the empty store. He was dreading the morning—not the bacon frying, donut stacking, coffee making parts, but them-the old love birds nested either in the motel or out at the ranch. No doubt, they would be up and out and staring at each other over coffee, or whatever, early in the morning again. *I guess they are so old they have to grab every opportunity,* he thought ruefully. It was the oddest Christmas gathering ever. And he'd participated in some very odd ones at the desert store. Like the one when Normaine cut down the plastic tree with a chain saw or the one when William married Algestine against everyone's wishes.

The grief part didn't go too badly, though. They all obviously missed Avery in their own ways. The trouble was, he'd been forced to sit through a room full of oldies that suddenly forgot their grief and started acting like a bunch of white-haired, (some dye jobs, of course, he expected that), young, teeny boppers intent on fun.

He'd ignored the maidenly blushes and the manly flushes crossing their old faces. They'd held hands openly. They'd murmured to each other. Susan and Perry. William and Lily Jean Bloome. Lana and Matthew. Six of 'em.

That was a bad number (according to his mother) and a bad sign. They drank wine, too. Way too much. Too late at night. They'd turned into a bunch of drunks intent on groping each other. He'd sent them out the doors—William and Lily Jean Bloome-Emma had made her escape in the store truck earlier-out the front door, Matthew, Lana, Susan, and Perry out the back door. He locked the doors behind them and quickly turned out the lights. He didn't wait to see which rooms they went to—each other's or their own. He didn't give a damn about that. Trouble was coming. He just knew it. He groaned. They were all guilty. Thank God he was heading back to California tomorrow morning. William and the rest were on their own.

www.ingramcontent.com/pod-product-compliance
Lightning Source LLC
Chambersburg PA
CBHW030617310726
48979CB00003B/763

* 9 7 8 1 7 3 5 6 2 6 6 0 4 *